## A STAR IS BORN

It was too horrible to be true. Taffy Sinclair and I have been worst enemies for practically our entire lives. We have even had clubs against each other. Actually you could say that our whole relationship has been like one long soap opera. But now, for Taffy Sinclair to get a part on a real soap, one that would be seen all over America, was just too much. I was so miserable I thought I'd die.

"*Interns and Lovers,* huh?" I grumbled. "Isn't that a hospital show? I hope she's playing a disease."

*Bantam Skylark Books by Betsy Haynes*
*Ask your bookseller for the books you have missed*

# TAFFY SINCLAIR, QUEEN OF THE SOAPS

Betsy Haynes

**BANTAM BOOKS**
NEW YORK · TORONTO · LONDON · SYDNEY · AUCKLAND

RL 6, 009–012

TAFFY SINCLAIR, QUEEN OF THE SOAPS

*A Bantam Skylark Book / June 1985*
*5 printings through May 1988*

*Skylark Books is a registered trademark of Bantam Books,*
*a division of Bantam Doubleday Dell Publishing Group, Inc.*
*Registered in U.S. Patent and Trademark Office and elsewhere.*

ISBN 0-553-15647-0

*Published simultaneously in the United States and Canada*

Bantam Books are published by Bantam Books, a division of Bantam
Doubleday Dell Publishing Group, Inc. Its trademark, consisting of the
words "Bantam Books" and the portrayal of a rooster, is Registered in
U.S. Patent and Trademark Office and in other countries. Marca
Registrada. Bantam Books, 666 Fifth Avenue, New York, New York 10103.

PRINTED IN THE UNITED STATES OF AMERICA

CW      14  13  12  11  10  9  8  7  6

*For Joe, my inspiration for Pink,*
*with love*

# 1 ✳

"**Y**OU'VE GOT TO BE KIDDING! NOT TAFFY SINCLAIR! NOT ON TELEVISION!" I knew I was shouting so loudly that every kid in the cafeteria was staring at me, but I couldn't help it. Not Taffy Sinclair. Not on television.

Taffy Sinclair is the world's most terrible person, as well as the snottiest and most stuck-up girl in Mark Twain Elementary. And that's not all. She isn't even normal. Taffy Sinclair's beautiful blond hair never frizzes. Her big blue eyes are never puffy or bloodshot. No spaghetti sauce or ball-point pen ink ever stains her gorgeous clothes. What's more, she has never had a zit in her life—and she doesn't even sweat! That's probably why the boys hang around her all the time. I guess I'd

1

have to admit that she's totally glamorous. So I really shouldn't have been so freaked-out when my best friend Beth Barry dropped the bomb.

I groaned and sat down with her and my three other best friends—Katie Shannon, Christie Winchell, and Melanie Edwards. Then I brightened up as a delicious thought struck me. "Is she going to appear on *Donahue* on a program about teenage pregnancy?" I asked with a smirk. "Or is she going to confess how drugs and booze have ruined her life?"

"Jana Morgan, you know perfectly well that Taffy Sinclair is too angelic to get involved in those kinds of things," said Melanie. Melanie swallows everything. Not just mountains of sweets, which account for her weight problem, but anything you tell her, which makes it fun to tell her things that are really bizarre.

"Of course! You're right. Why didn't I think of it?" I said, slapping my forehead with the heal of my hand. "She's going to impersonate Shirley Temple singing 'On the Good Ship Lollipop.'"

"Naw," piped up Christie. "She's playing Brooke Shields's part in the sequel to *The Blue Lagoon*."

We all started giggling like crazy, thinking of Taffy and her bust and how she's more developed than we'll ever hope to be. All of us were giggling, that is, except Beth. Her face was like a storm cloud. "That's okay," she said in her most dramatic voice. "If you don't want to know what she's really going to do on television, just go ahead and laugh like a bunch of idiots."

We shut up immediately.

Beth smiled wickedly, and then she kept us in suspense for a whole minute before she announced triumphantly, "She has a part in that soap opera *Interns and Lovers.*"

It was too horrible to be true. Taffy Sinclair and I have been worst enemies for practically our entire lives. We have even had clubs against each other. And once when my friends were mad at me, she pretended to be my best friend and teach me body language so I could send messages to cute boys. But that had been a disaster. Actually you could say that our whole relationship has been like one long soap opera. But now, for Taffy Sinclair to get a part on one, one that would be seen all over America, was just too much. I was so miserable I thought I'd die.

"*Interns and Lovers,* huh?" I grumbled. "Isn't that a hospital show? I hope she's playing a disease."

"*Interns and Lovers,*" Melanie repeated in a dreamy voice. "My mom watches that one every day. It's the only soap she absolutely refuses to miss. She won't even go to the bathroom while it's on."

"Well, I hate to tell you, but all the disease parts must be taken," said Beth. "Taffy has the part of a girl dying of leukemia."

I closed my eyes. I could see it all. There was Taffy lying pale and beautiful against mounds of snow-white pillows while half a dozen handsome doctors and interns hovered around her bed, taking her pulse and watching her eyelids flutter, murmuring, "She can't die now. She just can't!" It was totally disgusting.

"How do you know so much, anyway?" asked Katie, who had been uncharacteristically quiet through this whole conversation. Katie is not only the radical feminist of our group, but she can never resist putting her two cents in.

"Well…" Beth said, raising one eyebrow dramatically, "when Wiggins sent me to the office to turn in the attendance sheet, I just happened to hear Mr. Scott talking on the phone to Taffy's mother."

Christie has developed a monster crush on Mr. Scott, the new assistant principal. She always acts as if she has special privileges as far as he's concerned since her mother is principal of Mark Twain Elementary. She shot a poison-dart look at Beth. It was plain to see she hated being scooped about *anything* that had *anything* to do with Mr. Scott. Now it's one thing to have a crush on a teacher. (I know. I'll never forget dreamy Mr. Neal in fifth grade.) But Christie's been jealous of anyone who even speaks Mr. Scott's name out loud, ever since he personally returned her wallet, which she dropped on purpose just inside his office door.

"I only heard one side of the conversation," Beth went on, "but Mr. Scott was saying that it was okay that Taffy missed school today to try out for the part of a girl dying of leukemia on *Interns and Lovers,* and congratulating Mrs. Sinclair on Taffy's getting the part. He was also saying that of course it would be okay for Taffy to miss school three days next week to go from Bridgeport back into New York City on the commuter train for the filming." Then glancing casually toward Christie, who was absolutely fuming, she added, "He's certainly being extra nice to Taffy, don't you think?"

Christie came up off the bench like an erupting volcano and lunged across the table toward Beth. I threw myself between them, thinking how Beth could never resist upstaging everybody and being dramatic. It wasn't until they calmed down and I straightened up again that I realized my left elbow had been in Melanie's chocolate milk, and that the arm of my favorite white sweatshirt was totally gross. Not only that, I had squashed my lunch, which I keep hidden inside my sweatshirt. I hide it because Mom insists that I pack my cream cheese and jelly sandwich and other lunch stuff in these weird bags she bought. (Naturally she thinks they're cool.) They say JANA'S BAG in big red letters and are covered with about a hundred happy faces. They would be all right for a little kid, but if a sixth-grade boy saw me with one, I'd be so embarrassed that I'd die.

Anyway, there I sat in my gross sweatshirt with my lunch plastered to my stomach, feeling miserable about how Taffy Sinclair was going to be on *Interns and Lovers* and was probably going to become a television star while the rest of us were still small, insignificant sixth-graders, when I heard someone call my name.

"Jana, can I talk to you for a minute?"

Even though the voice was coming from behind me, I knew whose it was. I would have known that voice anywhere. It belonged to Randy Kirwan, the cutest boy in the whole sixth grade. But Randy isn't just cute (in spite of the fact that he has dark wavy hair and big blue eyes and is a super athlete). He's also a truly kind and sensitive person, and I'd been certain for a long time that he was starting to be just a little bit crazy about me. I would never forget the Halloween party a few weeks ago when he came dressed as a hunchback and hung around me most of the evening making monster noises. I know that some girls wouldn't think that was very romantic, but they don't know Randy. He has trouble expressing his feelings sometimes.

I turned around, trying to untangle my legs

from the lunch table bench and give him my best smile. "Sure, Randy," I said.

The next thing I knew, we were walking out of the cafeteria together. I wasn't the least bit self-conscious. I was remembering that once when I called him on the phone and disguised my voice so I could ask him how he really felt about me, he had said he would tell me when he was ready. I knew that was why he wanted to talk to me. He must be ready right now. I was so excited I thought I'd die.

# 2 *

I knew everybody was watching us as we walked out of the cafeteria. Every eye was on us, just as if we were a bride and groom leaving a church. I was so happy that I hardly even felt my lunch bouncing around inside my sweatshirt.

Randy stopped when we got into the hall. I stopped, too, flashing another smile, and waited to hear what he was going to say. I was looking into those kind eyes of his, and they were looking back at me.

Finally he tore his gaze away from mine and said, "Curtis Trowbridge wants you to meet him in the Media Center."

I was stunned. I could feel my ears starting to get hot, and it seemed like half an hour before I could make a sound. "Curtis Trowbridge?" I finally said, hoping Randy hadn't heard the catch in my voice. That was the last thing I had expected him to say. I looked down at my feet so he wouldn't see the disappointment on my face. Curtis Trowbridge was okay, I guess. I mean, I didn't think he was the nerd of the world anymore, but he's had a crush on me for ages, which is unfortunate because he's a genius and not very cool, and certainly not my type. Comparing him to Randy would be like comparing Alfred E. Neuman to Spider Man. I sighed. "What in the world does *he* want?"

"He said he wants to ask you something. He said it's important and he needs to ask you now, but he has to stay in the Media Center."

I ticked off the possibilities in my mind. He was probably building a rocket in there and wanted me to fly to the moon with him. Or maybe he thought it would be romantic for us to count to a billion together...by fives. That's the kind of genius he is.

Randy was waiting for an answer. I was trapped. There was only one thing I could say.

"Sure. I'll meet him. He probably forgot the social studies assignment or something."

"Gee, Jana, that's great. Not everybody is so nice to Curtis. He's really not a bad guy, you know. He can't help it if he's smart. Well, see you around."

Randy shoved through the door to the playground and was gone. I stood there thinking about what a kind and sensitive person he was for sticking up for Curtis Trowbridge. As disappointed as I was, I was glad I had told Randy I would talk to Curtis.

Then it hit me. Why hadn't I realized it before? Randy was putting me to the test to see if I am as kind and sensitive as he is. After all, if two people are going to be crazy about each other, they should have a lot of things in common. Randy really was crazy about me. He had just proved it!

I was so happy that it was all I could do to keep from running to the Media Center. I knew better than to run, though, because if I did, I'd be certain to get caught by Radar Rollins. Mr. Rollins teaches fourth grade, but during lunch period he patrols the halls looking for speeders. It's uncanny how he can turn a corner and spot a kid just as he starts to dash down a hall. That's how he got the nickname Radar.

Anyway, I didn't run and I didn't see Radar Rollins, and when I got to the Media Center, I found Curtis Trowbridge sitting at one of the big library tables poring over some old copies of the *Mark Twain Sentinel,* the world's most boring school newspaper. It wasn't always so boring, but this year Curtis was picked by the teachers to be the editor, which is supposed to be a big honor. The only trouble is that Curtis definitely does not have a flair for journalism. He reports exciting things like the new paint job in the boys' bathroom and the broken window in the cafeteria. I had a feeling he knew about his problem, because he had a worried look on his face, as if he'd just failed a math test or something.

I plopped down onto a chair across the table from him. "Hi, Curtis. What's up?"

"Oh, Jana, am I ever glad to see you." The worried look was gone. Now he was grinning like crazy. "I have just decided to make you a reporter and give you the opportunity to write great stories for the *Sentinel*. All you have to do is come up with a great story by the Friday afternoon deadline."

I had a funny feeling in the pit of my stomach. Curtis had already given me the chance to be a reporter for the *Sentinel*. He had given almost everybody in the sixth grade that chance, but everybody had turned him down. Besides, Friday afternoon was today. "What's the catch?" I asked.

"No catch, Jana. Honest." He was trying to keep the phony grin on his face but it was slowly drizzling down into a look of desperation. "Will you do it? Please?"

"But why me? Why not write a great story yourself and keep all the glory?"

"You're the one with the super imagination," he said hopefully. Then he sighed and added in a weak voice, "And all the...friends. Hardly anybody will even talk to me, but everybody talks to you." He sighed again and I couldn't help feeling a little bit sorry for him. "Actually the kids have been complaining about how boring the paper is and how much news I miss. Scott Daly was really mad last week because I didn't report that he won the free-throw contest in boys' gym. I was excused from gym last week because my glasses were broken, so I didn't know about the free-throw contest. How can I print news if nobody tells me about it?"

"Gee, Curtis. I'd like to help but..." There was a war going on inside my head. Curtis really was okay, and it made me mad sometimes the way some kids treated him. Still, what could I do? I didn't have any news.

"Not only that," he said. "Mr. Cagney is the faculty adviser for the paper, and he said that if I didn't do better"—Curtis paused and got a really embarrassed look on his face—"they would have to find someone else to be editor."

I was definitely starting to feel sorry for Curtis now. Like Randy had said, he wasn't a bad guy and he couldn't help being so smart. Curtis must have seen the indecision on my face, because he leaned closer and said, "If you come up with a great story, I'll even write it for you and still give you the by-line. That way everyone will see that I am a great editor and I have a great reporter, too!"

How do I get myself into these things? I couldn't

help asking myself that question as I tried to ignore a waspy little idea that kept buzzing around in my brain. *Buzz. Buzz. Buzz.* It was battering my skull to get out. I hated that waspy little idea. I couldn't. I wouldn't. Not even to help out a friend in need. What would my best friends think of me if I did?

But deep down I knew I had to do it. I had to put personal feelings aside. That's what Randy Kirwan would do, and we have so much in common. I took a deep breath. I swallowed hard. Then I took another deep breath and finally said, "I have a scoop for you, Curtis. A big one. Taffy Sinclair is going to be on television."

## 3 ✿

When we were walking home together after school, I didn't tell my four best friends what I had done. And when they asked why Randy Kirwan had called me out of the lunchroom, I lied and said he wanted to know something about an assignment. I didn't tell them over the weekend either. Actually I didn't even see them, because Mom was on a closet-cleaning binge. Usually I don't hang around for things like that but, number one, I was trying to avoid slipping up and admitting to my friends that I had told Curtis Trowbridge about Taffy Sinclair. We weren't even supposed to know about her, and I had broadcast the story to the entire school. Number two, Mom dug out a

14

box full of my baby pictures and let me take them to my room and look through them.

I suppose it sounds conceited, but I spent practically the whole weekend poring over those pictures. There were pictures of me when I was a newborn baby, pictures of me in my high chair pouring cereal over my head, pictures of me riding my tricycle, and all that kind of stuff.

But my favorites were the pictures of my third birthday. There was one picture of me sitting on Mom's lap hugging my new Big Bird doll and one of me sitting on my father's lap tearing the paper off a present. I was sorry that there wasn't just one photo of me with both of them, but Mom said there wouldn't have been anybody left to snap the picture. I wondered if that was really the reason or if they were just too mad at each other to be in the same picture, since it was not long after my third birthday that they got divorced.

I couldn't stop looking at that picture of me with my father. I haven't seen him since they split up, and he hardly ever writes. Then I discovered something funny. When I put the two pictures exactly side by side to make one picture, it looked like I was identical twins, and both Mom and Dad were in the picture. I have always wanted a twin, or at least a brother or sister. I liked that double picture so much that I taped the two halves together and hid it in the drawer where I keep my sweaters so that I could look at it whenever I wanted to.

Anyway, by Monday morning I was beginning to be sorry that I had told Curtis Trowbridge about Taffy. I kept hoping and praying that he would keep his mouth shut about where he got his information. After all, a good newpaperman protects his sources, and that was all I had been—just a source. I had hardly told him anything, except that Taffy Sinclair was going to be on television and that she had a teensy little part on the soap opera *Interns and Lovers*. I hoped he would forget that he'd said he would give me the by-line.

By the time I got to school, I was feeling pretty optimistic that I would get away with it. I was feeling that way until I caught sight of Taffy Sinclair. My friends and I were standing near the street watching three boys up by the side of the building where there aren't any windows. The boys were passing around a cigarette. While one of them puffed away like crazy, the other two kept watch for teachers. Then the next boy would take the cigarette, and so on. You could tell they thought they were pretty cool.

Anyway, I was so busy watching them that until she called my name, I didn't know Taffy Sinclair had come out the front door of the school and was standing on the top step as if she were on a stage. As usual, she looked absolutely perfect. Her blond hair was brushed back from her face, and she was wearing gorgeous burgundy corduroys, a gray sweater, and a matching burgundy and gray down vest. In my faded jeans and my New York Mets baseball jersey I had never felt more tacky.

"Jana! I've got to talk to you!" she yelled, and started toward me. I couldn't believe my eyes. She was smiling so big that you could see her one crooked bicuspid, the only flaw on her otherwise perfect body. Then she pulled some papers out of her notebook and started waving them around.

"What's the matter with her?" whispered Christie.

"Who knows?" I whispered back.

But as she got closer, I saw that the papers in her hand weren't just any papers. They were the *Mark Twain Sentinel,* mimeographed in that putrid shade of purple and stapled together.

"Oh, no," I groaned as she swooped down on us. She was still smiling and I had the terrible feeling I knew what was coming next.

I did.

"Oh, Jana. I'm so glad I stopped by school this morning to get my assignments before I go into the city for the filming," she gushed. "Mr. Scott gave me a copy of the *Sentinel* to take along with me and read on the train. Otherwise I wouldn't have know anything about this super story you wrote about me."

She shoved the paper so close to my nose that my eyes crossed, but just the same I couldn't help reading that headline.

## TAFFY SINCLAIR: QUEEN OF THE SOAPS

by
Jana Morgan

I sputtered something about not writing the story myself, but Taffy just kept on grinning and holding the paper up to my face. I could feel my friends all glaring at me. It was as if their eyes were laser beams, and they were boring into me. Not only that, but we were drawing a crowd. Kids from all over the school grounds were drifting over to see what was going on.

At that moment I thought things couldn't get any worse, but just then Taffy did a terrible thing. She whipped the paper around and started reading the article out loud.

"'Taffy Sinclair, the beautiful, blond-haired, blue-eyed sweetheart of the sixth grade, is about to become a big television star.'" Taffy read it in a really loud voice, emphasizing the words *beautiful* and *sweetheart*. It was so disgusting I thought I'd die. How could that nerd Curtis Trowbridge do a thing like this to me?

But Taffy wasn't finished yet. She stopped reading and looked at me with an icky sweet expression on her face. Deep down I was sure Taffy knew I hadn't written that story and she was enjoying seeing me squirm. "Really, Jana, I didn't know you were such a big fan of mine," she said. Then she put this innocent look on her face, which, of course, was fake, and asked, "Would you like my autograph?"

That did it. I went stomping across the school grounds as fast as I could. She really had her nerve. But then Taffy Sinclair was the most conceited person in the world. If there was an Olympic event for being conceited, Taffy would not only make the U.S. team, she would win the gold medal. I could hear her reading more of the story, so I covered my ears with my hands and started to run.

A minute later my four best friends came up behind me. "Jana, would you slow down and tell us what's going on?" demanded Katie. She looked really mad and she swung her thick red hair around her shoulders angrily.

"Yeah," said Melanie. She was frowning, too. "I can't believe you'd do Taffy such a big favor. I mean, with a story like that, you could just about become her publicity agent."

I stopped and turned around to face them. I hoped that they weren't really mad at me, that they were just confused. I could certainly understand that.

"First," I began. "I didn't write that story. You've

got to believe me, because it's true." Then I went on to tell them about Curtis and about how Mr. Cagney had said they would have to pick another sixth-grader to be editor if he didn't write more exciting stories. Then I crossed my fingers for luck and went on to tell them that in a moment of weakness I had given him a scoop. "I wasn't trying to do Taffy any favors," I said, and added what I hoped would be a big finish. "I only did it to help a friend in need."

Nobody said anything for a minute. Then Christie sort of shrugged and said, "Oh, well. Curtis deserves a little help, I guess, and everybody would have found out about Taffy anyway."

"Sure," said Beth. "She certainly wouldn't have kept it a secret."

"Besides," Melanie added hopefully. "According to the article, Taffy is introduced in the first episode, gets a lot worse in the second, and dies in the third. She isn't going to be a big television star for long."

Just then the first bell rang, and I was glad for it as I trudged off toward the school. But I could hear Taffy laughing and talking to all her new fans. I didn't look in her direction. I didn't want to give her that satisfaction. But looking straight ahead wasn't any better. There was that nerd Curtis Trowbridge marching toward me, his glasses bouncing on his nose.

"Just wait until you see the *Sentinel*," he said excitedly. Then he winked at me and wiggled his eyebrows like Groucho Marx. "I gave you your by-line just the way I promised, even though you didn't write the story. I don't mind sharing the glory with you, even though I did interview her and write it up. After all, it was your news tip."

All I could do was stare at him. He was such a jerk that he actually thought I wanted my name on that story and that I would fall madly in love with him if he gave me a by-line. No wonder he didn't have any friends.

"Thanks, Curtis," I mumbled, and brushed on past him. I knew there was no use telling him how I really felt. He was too much of a nerd to understand.

The rest of the day was pretty boring. Taffy left to go into New York City to film her soap, or her "daytime drama" as I heard her correct one of her fans. Mr. Scott brought around the *Sentinel*, to be handed out at the end of homeroom, and Christie turned red and almost fainted when he looked in her direction and smiled. That gave me an idea for another scoop. I could see the headline now:


## SIXTH–GRADER ELOPES WITH ASSISTANT PRINCIPAL

by
Jana Morgan

I had to chuckle to myself. Maybe the job of reporter wouldn't be so bad after all. I could keep my eye out for great stories and do interviews with sports heroes like Randy Kirwan. The more I thought about that idea, the more I liked it. Maybe Mom could give me some pointers. After all, she does work at the newspaper. She isn't a reporter, but she's the classified ad manager and she's pretty smart.

Anyway, all day long I kept wondering about Taffy Sinclair and the filming. Did she have a dressing room with a star on her door? Did she bring her own clothes or would they furnish her with a gorgeous wardrobe? Of course, since she was playing the part of a girl dying of leukemia, she probably wouldn't need a lot of changes. And what if she forgot her lines? Would they get mad and yell at her or would they just stop the cameras and shoot the scene all over again? I had millions of questions, but, of course, I would never ask her any of them. I'd die if she ever thought I was jealous.

After school I streaked home as fast as I could. Even though I hated Taffy Sinclair more than anybody I knew, I couldn't help myself. I had to watch the soap. I filled a bowl with chips, grabbed a can of soda, and flipped on the tube. I just made it in time, too, because at that instant, organ music swelled and across the screen flashed the words:

**INTERNS AND LOVERS**

# 4 ✿

After what seemed like a dozen commercials, the organ music came back, lingered on a quivery note for an instant, and the camera faded in on a hospital room and a dark-haired young woman lying in bed. She was staring sadly out the window, and beside her hung an upside-down bottle connected to a long tube and a needle stuck in her arm. Yuck! I thought. What you had to go through to be an actress.

The camera shot widened, taking in the door, but there was still no sign of Taffy Sinclair. Humph, I thought. Her part is probably so small that the audience won't even notice her. Just then the young woman in the hospital bed began to cry softly, and

24

as she reached for a tissue to wipe away her tears, the door burst open and the most gorgeous man I have ever seen in my life came into the room. He was huge and handsome with sun-streaked blond hair, but what really impressed me were his eyes. They were the bluest blue imaginable. But that's not all. They were kind and sensitive. I could tell right away that he was a truly kind and sensitive person, just like Randy Kirwan. I held my breath as he stopped at the foot of her bed, gazing down at her with those kind and sensitive eyes. Then he went to her side and clasped one of her hands in his. You could tell he was crazy about her, and when he started speaking, I forgot all about Taffy Sinclair.

*"Cynthia, my darling. Oh, Cynthia. What have you done to yourself?"*

*"Chad! How did you ever find me?"*

*"That doesn't matter now. What matters is you. Look at yourself. You're skin and bones. You've lost so much weight that you look like a tiny frail bird."*

*"You don't understand, Chad. I really need to take off a few more pounds. Doctor Norris is being absolutely awful about it. He put me into the hospital and he's treating me like a prisoner. Oh, Chad. You've got to help me get out of here."*

I watched in horror as Cynthia sat up and tried to get out of bed. Chad was right. She was pretty

skinny. But she was also weak. She stumbled, fall-
ing into Chad's strong arms. Thank goodness he
was standing so close. But, of course, someone like
Chad would always be there when you needed
him. He lifted her gently and put her back into
bed and she lay there looking pale and exhausted.
Just then the camera zeroed in on his face where
the look of love that had been in his eyes only a
moment ago had been replaced by fear.

*"Cynthia, my love. You have to realize that your desire
to lose weight is really a sickness, a sickness known as
anorexia. Doctor Norris explained it all to me. He said
that you're wasting away and that if you don't start eating
again . . . you'll die."*

I held my breath. What would Cynthia do now?
Surely she wouldn't let herself die when Chad
loved her so much. Nobody would. She'd have to
be crazy. I could hardly wait to hear what she
would say next.

But instead of moving to Cynthia, the camera
stayed on Chad, and the angle widened as he
moved away from her toward a second bed in the
room. At first I didn't understand what was
happening, but then I saw that someone was lying
in that second bed. It was Taffy Sinclair! And she
was in the very same room with kind and sensitive
Chad. I thought I'd die.

My throat tightened as Chad tiptoed over to

Taffy's bed, looking down at her as if his heart would break.

"*Look at this poor, beautiful girl, Cynthia. Doctor Norris tells me she's dying of leukemia. I know she would give anything to have your chance for life.*"

The camera cut to Taffy in a mint-green nightie lying pale and beautiful on her mound of pillows, just the way I had imagined, but instead of worried doctors and interns hovering around her, it was Chad. I felt like throwing up. Taffy's eyes were closed, and a single tear was glistening on her cheek. I grunted in disgust. It probably wasn't a real tear, but just a drop of water flicked onto her cheek by a prop man while the camera was on Chad and Cynthia. But Chad didn't know that. He was taken in by Taffy. He thought it was a real tear. You could tell by the tender way he was looking at her. I wished I could shout to him and tell him what a truly horrible person Taffy Sinclair really is.

Then Cynthia started talking again, and the camera swung away from Taffy and onto her.

"*You don't understand. I don't want to die. I just want to be thin and beautiful and have some discipline and self-control in my life.*"

"*Very well, Cynthia. If you are determined to destroy yourself, I can't stop you.*" Chad turned and walked to the door, where he paused and looked back at her. The camera closed in on his pain-filled face. *"But without you I have no reason to live."*

The organ music swelled again, and Chad's face dissolved into mist as a bunch of commercials paraded across the screen. I looked nervously at my watch. Ten minutes to go before the end of the show. Surely Cynthia wouldn't let Chad do anything desperate, but she was so weak. Could she stop him in just ten minutes?

The commercials seemed to last forever, but finally the cameras were on Cynthia again. I couldn't believe that she was still lying in bed staring out the window the way she had been at the start of the show. Why wasn't she doing something? Hadn't she heard what Chad said? Didn't she believe him? She must have heard my questions because she began talking to herself.

*"He's only bluffing. I know he's only bluffing. Chad would never take his own life. Never."*

Just then I heard another sound. It was sirens and they were getting louder. My heart began to pound. Was Chad all right? I leaned closer to the television set as a nurse ran into the room. She looked scared to death and she ran straight to Cynthia.

*"He's on the roof. That handsome young man who was in here just now. He's on the roof, and he's threatening to jump!"*

The scene faded, ending the show for the day and leaving me paralyzed on the sofa. I sat there for a long time. I didn't even change the channel when a stupid cartoon came on. All I could think about was Cynthia. How could she be such a jerk? How could she just lie there when kind and sensitive and wonderful Chad was about to jump off the hospital roof? I was so worried about Chad I almost cried.

Then I thought about Randy Kirwan. He and Chad had a lot in common, even though Chad had blond hair and Randy's hair was dark. I would never let Randy jump off a hospital roof. He wouldn't even have to beg me to eat. I'd do anything to save his life. I closed my eyes. I could see it all.

"Jana, my darling, Oh, Jana, what have you done to yourself?"

"Randy! How did you ever find me?"

"That doesn't matter now. What matters is you. Look at yourself. You're skin and bones. You've lost so much weight that you look like a tiny frail bird. If you don't start eating again...you'll die. Promise me that you'll eat something. Otherwise I'll jump off the roof."

"Of course, Randy darling. I'll eat anything to save you."

"Sauerkraut?"

"Yes. Even sauerkraut."

"Liverwurst?"

But before I could answer him, I heard another sound. Was it sirens? My heart began to pound. No, it was only the phone.

# 5 ✱

*I*t was Beth.

"So what did you think of Taffy Sinclair?" she demanded.

I gulped. In my concern over Chad and Randy I had practically forgotten about Taffy Sinclair. But now I remembered that fake tear on her cheek and how taken-in Chad had been.

"She was so sickening I almost threw up," I blurted out.

"So did I. She was totally disgusting."

"Totally!"

"'Look at this poor, beautiful girl,'" Beth mimicked in her best theatrical voice. "Poor? YUCK! Beautiful? YUCK!"

"Puke!"

"Regurgitate!"

"Vomit!"

We both started making throwing-up noises and laughing. We got so carried away that after a couple of minutes I was gagging and thought I might really throw up, but luckily I didn't.

When we finally calmed down, I asked Beth if she wanted to watch *Interns and Lovers* at my house tomorrow. She said yes, so I called Christie, Katie, and Melanie and asked them and they said yes, too. I thought it was a good idea for us to watch together. That way if any of us got sick to our stomachs over Taffy Sinclair's disgusting performance, the others would be there to help. Good grief! I thought. What if we all got sick? The living room would look like a hospital ward.

At that moment the front door opened. An instant later it slammed so hard that the pictures rattled on the walls. Mom was home. I cringed. Where could I hide?

Mom and I usually get along fairly well, but that week the mere thought of Mom coming home from work filled me with terror. She'd been in a disgusting mood. I was sure it had something to do with Pink. Pink is short for Wallace Pinkerton, and he's Mom's boyfriend. At least he used to be. He's a printer at the same newspaper where Mom is the classified ad manager, and they have lunch together every day and dinner at our house a couple of nights a week. Every Saturday night Pink takes Mom bowling. He's an absolute bowling nut. But last Saturday night Pink brought Mom home early—so early I was still up watching TV. Mom stormed in the door muttering something about "that hussy at the bowling alley" and headed straight to bed. She's been a holy terror ever since.

"Jana," she roared. She looked so mad that I wouldn't have been surprised to see her breathing fire and smoke. "What are you doing watching TV at this hour of the day? Is your homework finished? And look at this apartment. It's a wreck!"

"I was on my way to do my homework now," I lied and made a beeline for my room. I started to tell her about Taffy Sinclair being on television and then decided she wasn't in the mood to be told anything. The best thing was just to stay out of her way.

I should have known that everyone at school would be talking about Taffy Sinclair the next day. But I didn't think of it. If I had, I would have invented an excuse to stay home. It was sickening. My four best friends thought so, too.

"Can you believe all this?" Christie was standing beside my locker looking exasperated. "Kids who hate Taffy Sinclair just as much as we do are going around acting like she's their best friend."

"I just overheard Clarence Marshall telling a

bunch of guys that he kissed her at Scott Daly's pool party last summer," said Katie.

"That's a laugh," I said. "Clarence Marshall is such a drip I'll bet he didn't even get invited to the pool party, much less kiss Taffy Sinclair." Suddenly a picture flashed into my mind. I could see chubby Clarence Marshall hauling himself out of the pool after a gigantic belly flop. His hair is plastered to his forehead, and his loud Hawaiian print trunks almost don't make it out of the water with him. Suddenly he dashes madly for Taffy Sinclair, puckers up, and plants a sloppy kiss right on her lips. Taffy's eyes fill with horror and she stares at him as if he were the Creature from the Black Lagoon. "On second thought," I said, "it would serve her right if he did."

We all laughed so hard at that that I didn't even see Randy Kirwan until he was standing beside me.

"Hi, Jana," he said, and smiled. I jumped as if I had just sat on a tack. I felt a little shiver start to travel through me. "Did you see Taffy Sinclair on television yesterday?"

The shiver fizzled out. So Randy had been taken in by Taffy's pitiful expression and fake tear, too. How could he and Chad be so gullible?

"No," I lied. "I have far more important things to do than sit around watching soap operas. Only gullible people believe what they see on them anyway."

"You're probably right," said Randy. "I was at football practice, so I didn't see her either. I just wondered how she did. You know, if she forgot her lines or anything."

"She didn't have any lines." The instant the words left my lips, I felt my ears getting hot. How could I have said such a stupid thing? I had just told him I didn't see the show.

"That's right," piped up Beth. "I called Jana right after it was over and told her all about it."

I shot her a grateful look as the first bell rang, and the conversation ended. The hall was suddenly filled with kids pushing and shoving their way to class. It was absolute bedlam with lockers banging and kids yelling. But I didn't mind. All that mattered was that Randy Kirwan had not been taken in by Taffy Sinclair after all. He hadn't even watched the program. And he agreed with me that only gullible people believed what they saw on soaps.

When my friends and I got to my house after school, I filled the bowl with chips again and got us each a can of soda. Everybody started munching and slurping away except Melanie. That was a surprise. I couldn't believe that she was on a diet. I wondered if she was sick. But I didn't think about it for long.

"Don't forget," I shouted. "Today Taffy gets a lot worse, and tomorrow..." I ran my finger across my throat and made a slashing sound.

We started hooting and cheering and clapping our hands, getting potato chip crumbs all over the place.

"That probably means she won't get to say any lines," I added. "She'll be too weak. In fact, she'll probably be too weak to cry any more fake tears."

Everybody agreed, and we were in pretty good spirits when I turned on the TV and flipped the dial to the right channel for *Interns and Lovers*. I settled back, thinking how much fun it was going to be to watch Taffy Sinclair waste away.

The first scene faded in. It was a nurses' station in the hospital. A nurse was sitting behind the desk looking down at some papers. A doctor stood to one side reading a patient's chart. All was quiet.

Suddenly another doctor came running up the hall so fast his white coat was flapping. *"It's a miracle! That's all it can be...a MIRACLE!"*

The nurse looked up and so did the doctor reading the chart. It's Chad, I thought. It has to be Chad. He's come down off the roof. They've saved him. But how? Did Cynthia finally eat? Did they carry her up to the roof so she could polish off a burger and fries in front of him? Why didn't the doctor explain?

After what seemed like the longest pause in

history, he raised a hand for the others to listen. I held my breath. My heart was pounding. What was he going to say?

The camera zoomed in for a close-up of his face. It was positively glowing. *"She's going to live! The girl with leukemia is going to live—and she's going to get well! Hurry! Come to her room! She's sitting up!"*

Everybody from the nurses' station went tearing down the hall, following the doctor in the flappy white coat. It was a regular stampede. When they crowded into the hospital room, Taffy Sinclair was sitting up in bed. She had a pitiful little smile on her face and another fat fake tear on her cheek.

The organ music thundered as the station cut away for a commercial, leaving my friends and me dumbfounded in front of the set.

## 6 ✱

"**W**hat happened?" I gasped as soon as I got my voice back. "She was supposed to get worse today and die tomorrow. Everybody knows that. Taffy said so herself."

"Maybe somebody goofed and accidentally got the wrong script," offered Beth.

"Maybe Taffy's mother paid off the network," said Christie. Leave it to Christie to think of money since she is a mathematical genius and plans to become an accountant someday.

Melanie had a dreamy look on her face. "I'll bet I know what happened. I'll bet Chad fell madly in love with Taffy and threatened to *really* jump off the roof if they let her die."

"Oh, for goodness' sake!" shrieked Katie. She jumped up off the sofa as if she had just fallen into a bed of cactus. She started pacing the floor, and I knew we were in for another one of her famous lectures. "How can all of you get so carried away with such a stupid sexist program? The characters are all stereotypes. Taffy and that Cynthia person are weak, helpless females. And Chad the Magnificent, the King of the Jungle, is supposed to save the day."

"Not if he jumps off the roof," I sang in a sarcastic voice, and we all started to giggle.

Katie looked as if she might explode, but just then the commercials ended and there he was, Chad the Magnificent, the King of the Jungle, poised on the edge of the roof. He was about four stories above the ground. Even Katie couldn't help but watch.

Chad had a tormented look on his face as if he had nothing left to live for. It broke my heart to see him like that. In the street below him police cars screeched to a stop and uniformed officers poured out. One of them shouted up to Chad through a bullhorn.

*"Unlock the door to the roof and come down. We want to help you."*

I held my breath. Surely he wouldn't jump. "He has so much to live for," I murmured. "There are lots of other women in the world besides Cynthia."

"Yeah," growled Christie. "There's always Taffy Sinclair."

I tried not to think about Taffy and Chad. I'd worry about that later—after Chad got down off the roof. The policeman was shouting at him again, but Chad didn't seem to hear him. He was staring into space as if his mind were a million miles away. Now a fire engine had joined the police cars, but Chad wasn't paying any attention to that either. Suddenly a look of surprise crossed his face, and his eyes widened in horror. The camera cut away, and we could see what Chad was looking at.

"That man!" I shouted. He's sneaking up behind that old lady!" Sure enough, a sleazy-looking guy was creeping up behind a white-haired lady with a pocketbook dangling from her arm. The police didn't even see it. They were all too busy trying to get Chad off the roof. Now that man was gaining on the old woman.

"Oh, my gosh," gasped Christie. "He's going to mug her."

We held our breaths as the camera swung back to Chad. He was waving his arms and shouting down to the policemen. *"Look behind you! There's a mugging going on!"*

Now the camera was on the policeman with the bullhorn. He squinted up at Chad. It was plain to see that he was too far away from Chad to hear what he was saying, and he began shouting orders to his men.

*"He's flipping out up there. Quick. Get the fire net. I think he's going to jump."*

Firemen in black-and-yellow striped coats came pouring off the engine. They hauled out the net and held it like a gigantic trampoline. Chad stopped waving and shouting. He stood perfectly still for an instant and then did a swan dive over the side of the building.

I could hear somebody screaming. I think it was me. I couldn't believe it. Chad had jumped!

"They caught him! He's alive! He's alive!" screamed Melanie. She grabbed me and hugged me until I couldn't breathe. Chad really was alive. He bounced a couple of times in the net and then scrambled to the edge and jumped over the side, racing through the police line to tackle the sleazy man just as he grabbed for the old lady's purse.

"He's a hero!" shouted Beth, and we started jumping up and down and shouting with her, "He's a hero! Chad's a hero!"

When we finally settled down, I noticed two things. One, the program had ended for the day and a cartoon was coming on. Two, Katie was still sitting down, and she had a disgusted look on her face.

"Good old Chad the Magnificent, the King of

the Jungle," she said in her most sarcastic voice. "Sexist, stereotype Chad saved the day just like I told you he would."

Leave it to Katie, I thought, to put a damper on things.

I sat in front of the TV for a long time after my friends left, but I wasn't really watching. I was thinking about Chad and how wonderful he was. He was not only kind and sensitive, but he was a genuine hero. I was also thinking about Randy Kirwan and how much he and Chad had in common. I was really glad that I had started watching *Interns and Lovers,* because it was helping me to understand things about people that I had never thought of before. Take Randy, for example. I knew now that he would never hesitate to jump off a roof to save an old lady from being mugged. He was kind and sensitive and he was a hero. I might not have known that if I hadn't started watching the show. And I had found out something about myself, too. I would eat anything, no matter how disgusting and gross, to save Randy. I closed my eyes and saw his face and those kind and sensitive eyes, and I felt tingly all over.

Then I saw another face. It was Taffy Sinclair's. I had learned something about her, too. You could never trust her. *I* had known that all along, of course, but here it was for the rest of the world to see. If you couldn't trust her to die when she was supposed to, how could you trust her for anything else?

Suddenly I got this great idea. It was plain that watching *Interns and Lovers* was making me more sensitive and helping me to understand the people around me. Maybe I should watch some other soaps, too. I grabbed the newspaper and turned to the TV schedule. *To Have and to Hold* was on another channel and following that was *To Live, Perchance to Love.* Mom wouldn't be home for a while, and when I heard her coming, I could race to my room and act like I was doing my homework.

I sat glued to the set for the next hour in a tube trance. In *To Have and to Hold* Samantha is engaged to Michael, who is almost as handsome as Chad. Her best friend is Terri, who is secretly trying to steal Michael away from her. Michael takes Samantha home from a date and then goes to a rendezvous on the beach with Terri, where they kiss while the waves crash against the rocks. Meanwhile Samantha calls her mother long-distance to announce that Michael told her he loves her. I couldn't help thinking that Michael was a real jerk to sneak around on Samantha like that. He certainly had nothing in common with Randy Kirwan, even though I had to admit he was awfully cute.

Then *To Live, Perchance to Love* came on. I could tell right away that Dierdre is a real villain. She's icky sweet to everybody, and she gets a really mean look in her eyes when nobody is noticing, and tells lie after lie about poor Julie, who suffered amnesia after being run over in a hit-and-run accident. Julie doesn't remember that she is married to Arthur, who is in jail for the hit-and-run accident but didn't cause it. Poor Arthur, I thought, and poor Julie.

I sat there for a few minutes after the program ended, trying to imagine what it would feel like not to remember anything, but I couldn't. Every time I tried not to remember something, I always did.

Still, I can't remember very many things that happened when I was really little. Oh, I remember some things. I remember one day when I was playing with another little girl in a kiddie pool in the backyard, but I can't remember who she was or if I ever played with her again. I remember that day because I stepped on a bee and got stung. And I remember being scared to death to sit on Santa's lap, and things like that. But I can't remember my father no matter how hard I try, and I try awfully hard sometimes. That makes me feel pretty sad. Maybe that was how poor Julie felt.

# 7❖

*T*affy Sinclair was waiting for my friends and me when we got to school the next morning. She had already gathered a big crowd of kids by the front steps.

"Would you look at Mona Vaughn," grumbled Christie.

I looked. It was disgusting. Poor, ugly Mona was gazing at Taffy as if she were some kind of rock star. The sad thing is that Taffy treats Mona like dirt most of the time, only letting her hang around when there's nobody else to talk to.

"How disgusting," I said. But Mona wasn't the only one. A few other girls were there, sort of hanging back as if they were afraid to talk to her. But the really disgusting thing was all the boys.

45

There were bunches of them, and it was plain to see that Taffy was enjoying all the attention. Taffy doesn't usually get that much attention since she's so snotty and stuck-up. Anyway, with all those boys crowded around her, it took me a minute to see if Randy Kirwan was there. Thank goodness he wasn't, but there was Clarence Marshall with a dopey grin on his face and Mark Peters and Scott Daly.

"Maybe we should sneak around to the back of the school before she sees us and go in through the gym," said Melanie. But she was too late. Taffy had spotted us.

"Jana! Katie! Beth!" she called. "Melanie! Christie! Guess what?"

"Who cares?" muttered Katie.

Taffy wasn't taking any chances on our getting away. She was headed toward us like a queen, with her court following behind. I would have welcomed an earthquake right about then so that the ground would have opened up and swallowed my friends and me. But no such luck.

"So many people called the network after my first appearance on *Interns and Lovers* wanting me to live, that when I got to the station for the filming yesterday, they had rewritten the script. Isn't that wonderful?"

"Yeah," added Clarence Marshall, "they all kept saying, 'You just can't let that *beautiful* girl die!,' didn't they, Taffy?" He was positively drooling.

Taffy was smiling at us with a poison-dart look in her eyes. She knew she had us squirming, but I'd die before I'd let her think we were jealous.

"Gee, Taffy," I said, trying to make my voice sound really sad. "Does that mean you'll have to quit school at Mark Twain Elementary and move to New York City?"

She didn't answer for a minute, but it was obvious that I had asked the question she wanted to hear. I didn't know why at first. I hadn't meant to do a thing like that.

"No, of course not," she said in an icky sweet voice just like the icky sweet voice that villain Deirdre uses in *To Live, Perchance to Love*. It made me want to throw up. "I'll only be on the show three days a week; I'll be at school the other two." She paused a minute and looked straight at Christie before she dropped the bomb. "The two days I'm here, I'll stay after so that Mr. Scott can tutor me. He'll tutor me on Saturday mornings, too."

I knew I should come to Christie's rescue and say something really brilliant, but I couldn't. Instead, I was seeing a picture in my mind. It was Taffy and Mr. Scott. They were all alone on Bridgeport Beach. There were papers and books beside them on the sand, but they weren't paying any attention to them. They were looking at each other just the way Terri and Michael looked at each other when they had their rendezvous on the beach in *To Have and to Hold.* Just as a wave crashed against the rocks and Taffy and Mr. Scott moved toward each other to kiss, I felt a jab in my ribs.

"What's the matter with you, Jana?" screamed Christie. "Did you go to sleep or something? Didn't you hear what she said?"

Taffy and her group of followers had moved on to capture some other unsuspecting kids, and Christie was standing next to me, fists clenched, looking as if she had come unglued. I certainly couldn't tell her about Taffy and Mr. Scott kissing on the beach. I had to think fast.

"Of course, I heard what Taffy said. But I didn't want to give her the satisfaction of thinking I cared. It's time for the bell. We'll talk about it more at lunch."

Christie was quiet at lunch. I knew why, but I couldn't think of anything to say. Melanie was quiet, too. And that's not all. The only things she had brought for lunch were a hard-boiled egg and an apple. That wasn't like her. And yet the more I thought about it, the more I realized that it had been ages since she had brought any of her mother's brownies to share at lunch. She used to bring her mother's brownies all the time. She also used to eat most of them. I wondered if her mother was sick.

"Melanie, is your mother sick?"

Melanie looked really surprised, and suddenly I noticed that she was a little thinner.

"Of course not. What would make you ask a thing like that?"

"Well, for one thing, that's a funny lunch," I said, pointing to her apple and hard-boiled egg. "And it's been weeks since you brought brownies to school."

"Jana Morgan, you dope," she said. "I'm on a diet. That's all."

"But why?" I asked. I had the sinking feeling that I knew what the answer would be. I could see now that she was more than just a little thin. She was getting absolutely skinny.

"I really need to take off some weight."

I stared at her, my mouth open, and when I didn't say anything, she shrugged.

"It's no big deal. All it takes is some discipline and self-control."

That did it. *Discipline. Self-control.* Those were Cynthia's words. She had said them the day Chad tried to get her to eat. I closed my eyes. I imagined Melanie lying in a hospital bed. She was skin and bones. She had lost so much weight that she looked like a tiny frail bird. Poor Melanie. She wasn't just losing weight. She was anorexic! What would happen to her? If Chad couldn't help Cynthia, what on earth could I do for Melanie?

Even though I knew Taffy Sinclair wouldn't be on *Interns and Lovers* today since she had been in school, I hurried home to watch it anyway. For Melanie's sake I had to find out more about anorexia. And I couldn't help wondering what would happen to Cynthia now that Chad was off the roof. Would she be so grateful he was safe that she would gobble up everything in sight and get well? That would give me hope for Melanie. The instant the show came on, I knew the answer.

The organ music was trembly as the camera focused on Cynthia lying in bed. She looked even worse than she had the day before. There were dark circles under her eyes, and her cheeks were so sunken that I wondered if she was sucking them in. A minute later Chad came into the room.

Cynthia tried to smile, but the corners of her mouth were just too weak to turn up very far. *"Chad,"* she whispered. *"My hero. I heard about how you saved that elderly lady from being mugged. I even saw it on TV."*

Chad shook his head sadly. *"I didn't come to talk about me. I've just had a conference with Doctor Norris. The prognosis is grim. He doesn't think he can save you now."* Chad's handsome face crumpled in sorrow, and he began to cry softly. My heart was in my throat. I couldn't stand to see Chad cry. If only there were something I could do.

Cynthia spoke up again, and this time her voice was stronger. *"Chad, there is something I desperately need to talk about. It's terribly important. Will you listen?"*

*"Of course, my darling. Anything. What is it?"*

The camera zoomed in on Cynthia, who sighed deeply before she spoke. *"There is one part of my life that you have never known about. When I was just a tiny child my parents divorced. My mother took good care of me and loved me very much, but my father ... my father never came to see me after that and almost never wrote. I felt sometimes as if he had forgotten I existed."*

I sat up straight as a poker. I couldn't believe it. I couldn't believe that somewhere in this world was another father like mine. Poor Cynthia. I knew just how she felt.

Cynthia brushed away a tear and went on. *"A few days ago, when I realized that I might not get well, I decided to make one last attempt at contacting my father. Today I got a response."*

She reached to her bedside table for a letter. My heart was pounding so hard it sounded like thunder. I couldn't watch, but I couldn't move away either.

*"Chad, it says here that I have an identical twin sister I never knew about. It says that when Dad and my mother decided to divorce they agreed that one of us would stay with each of them. That way, both of them would still have a child. They decided that it would be best if neither of us knew the other existed. That's why he never came to see me and only wrote me once in a while."*

I sank back against the sofa. I could feel little explosions going off in my heart. An identical twin sister. That's why he never came to see her and hardly ever wrote. Suddenly I couldn't sit there any longer. I jumped up off the sofa and went tearing into my room. I jerked open my sweater drawer and pulled out that picture of my third birthday. There I was, sitting on Mom's lap on one side of the picture and my father's lap on the other. But was I? Were they both really me? I couldn't take my eyes off that picture. I was so excited I thought I'd die.

## 8 ✻

Could that be why my father never came to see me and hardly ever wrote? Was he too busy taking care of my secret identical twin? Suddenly I was very grateful to *Interns and Lovers*. I might never have suspected my twin existed if I hadn't started watching the show. I was even a little grateful to Taffy Sinclair.

My hands were shaking so hard that I had to put the picture down on my desk to study it. The little girls on both sides of the photograph looked like the same person, but, of course, identical twins always do. That's why they're called identical. They usually comb their hair alike and dress alike and everything. Still, I looked for some little tell-tale difference, like a scraped knee on one of them

53

or something, anything that would prove that they weren't the same person, but there was nothing like that there.

After a minute I went to my full-length mirror, staring hard at myself and thinking that this was what it would be like to look at my twin. That gave me a tingly feeling.

"Hi," I said to my pretend twin in the mirror. Then I smiled and, of course, she smiled back. I closed my eyes and tried to remember back to when I was really little. Was there somebody else in our family, another little kid like me? My mind was blank. I could sort of remember the girl in the kiddie pool that day, but I didn't know if she was related to me or if she was just a neighbor. Could she have been my twin? I sighed. If I couldn't remember my father, how could I hope to remember my twin?

Still, I *could* have an identical twin. If I did, was she as much like me on the inside as she was on the outside? Did she take cream-cheese-and-jelly sandwiches in her lunch? Would she like my friends? And what about Randy Kirwan? Would she be able to see how kind and sensitive he is? I felt a funny little stab in my heart when I thought about my twin and Randy Kirwan. What if he met her someday and decided he liked her better than me?

And I couldn't help wondering about Mom and

my father. Did Mom miss my twin? Did she think about her often? I gulped as tears filled my eyes. Did my father miss me?

I looked at the picture again, but even though my twin was right in front of me, she seemed far away. I had to find out more about her. I just had to. I thought about asking Mom, but I couldn't do that. I'd die if I asked her and she started to cry. Besides, if I was wrong about this, she'd probably think I'd gone crazy.

Just then the phone rang.

"Hello?" I growled the word so that whoever it was would know they interrupted something important.

"Jana, did you watch *Interns and Lovers?*" It was Beth. "Isn't it exciting? Cynthia has a twin!"

"Sure, I watched," I said. I felt sort of guilty, as if I had been caught spying on someone.

"Can you *imagine* what it would feel like to find out you had an identical twin sister who'd been kept secret from you all your life?"

I opened my mouth to say something, but my heart was in my throat. I wanted to tell Beth that I might have a twin sister and that I sort of knew how it felt. After all, Beth Barry was my very best friend. But I couldn't. It was all too personal and private right now to tell even my best friend.

"What do you think Cynthia will do now?" Beth

asked, not waiting for me to answer her. "I bet she'll eat. I bet she'll get well now so she can go visit her twin. Wouldn't that be exciting?"

"Sure" was all I could say. I hadn't thought about Cynthia visiting her twin. I hadn't thought about visiting my twin, either. I wanted to hang up so I could think about it. But I had no sooner put down the phone than it rang again.

"Jana!" It was Christie, and she was positively shrieking. "Can you come over right now? I'm going to call everybody else. You've got to come. It's important!"

"What's so important that I have to come now? I haven't even started my homework." That was the truth, but secretly I also wanted to think about my twin some more.

"It's about Taffy Sinclair. I knew she'd be staying after school today so Mr. Scott could tutor her, so I stayed after, too. I hung around Mom's office and right by his office when Taffy came in. You should have seen the way she was batting her eyes and flirting with him!"

"So what's new about Taffy Sinclair batting her eyes and flirting, and why does everybody have to come over to your house?" I asked. I still didn't understand. I knew Christie was fuming over Mr. Scott, but Taffy did that sort of thing all the time.

"We're going to fix her once and for all," said

Christie. "Just come over and bring your notebook from the Against Taffy Sinclair Club."

That was all I needed to hear. Wild horses couldn't have kept me away from Christie's house. I wrote Mom a note explaining where I was and started rummaging around in my closet for my Against Taffy Sinclair Club notebook. We had each started a notebook last year in fifth grade when we had our club against Taffy, and we had used them to record all the mean, snotty, and truly horrible things she did. I hadn't seen mine in a long time. Not since I used some pages in it to make lists of my friends' faults that time when we were all mad at one another. Finally I found it under a big pile of stuff. I grabbed it and headed for the door. I paused beside my mirror, but I didn't look. I knew my twin would understand.

I was the last one to get to Christie's house, and she practically dragged me through the door and into the kitchen, where our meeting was apparently going to be held. She had pulled an extra chair up to the kitchen table so that all five of us could sit down, and she had set a mug full of pencils in the middle.

"What is this, school?" I asked when Christie left the room for a minute.

"Who knows? I think she's flipped out," said Beth, making a weird face.

Katie shook her head and frowned as if it were all beyond her, but Melanie only shrugged. I stared at Melanie. She was getting thinner and thinner. She was probably too weak from her anorexia to say anything.

A minute later Christie charged back into the room. She clutched a folded newspaper in one hand, her Against Taffy Sinclair Club notebook in the other. A triumphant look was on her face.

"Okay, everybody. Let's get started," she barked. "Remember when we had our self-improvement club called The Fabulous Five?"

I nodded. Everybody else nodded, too.

"Remember all the problems we had and how mad we got when each of us told the others their worst faults?"

Who could forget a thing like that? I thought. But before any of us could nod again, Christie went on. "And most of all, remember what we decided to do after we stopped being mad and made up again?"

"To let people see us for what we really are," I said. There were nods and murmurs of agreement around the table.

Christie didn't say anything for a minute. I didn't know if she was giving us time for the idea to sink in or if she was just trying to be dramatic like Beth. Either way I couldn't see what it had to do with Taffy flirting with Mr. Scott.

"Exactly!" she said finally. "And now it's time to take that idea one step further. It's time to do the same thing for Taffy Sinclair."

"You mean, to let people see Taffy for what she really is?" I asked. "How are we going to do a thing like that?"

A wicked grin spread across Christie's face. "Not *we*, Jana. *You!*" She was pointing her finger at me. "*You* are the reporter for the *Mark Twain Sentinel. You* are the one who is trying to help Curtis Trowbridge by getting exciting stories into the *Sentinel,* and *you* can get an exposé about Taffy Sinclair into next week's paper, just like the exposés they print in the *National Enquirer.*" Christie whipped the folded newspaper into the air and held it up for us to see. It was the *National Enquirer,* all right.

"What's an exposé?" asked Melanie in a weak voice.

"It's a disgusting article full of lies about an innocent person," said Katie.

"It's an article about a celebrity who acts goody-goody and perfect in front of everybody, but does terrible things in private," corrected Christie. "It exposes what that person is really like so everyone can see her for what she really is."

"I don't want my by-line on a thing like that," I said. I was beginning to feel trapped, even though I'd have to admit that an exposé of Taffy Sinclair sounded like a pretty good idea.

"Put Curtis Trowbridge's by-line on it. He's such a jerk he won't know the difference," said Christie. "Besides, Curtis's grandfather died all the way out in California, and he's going to be absent for more than a week to go to the funeral. He'll never even know about the story. And Taffy probably won't know about it until the day after it comes out and everybody has already read it. Remember, she went into the city to be on television last Monday, so she'll probably go in this Monday, too."

The more I thought about writing an exposé of Taffy Sinclair, the better I liked the idea. She certainly deserved it. And if I could turn the story in with Curtis Trowbridge's by-line on it, I could get revenge on Taffy for all the truly mean and horrible things she has done to me, and nobody would know that I had written it. Not to mention that I could get back at Curtis for putting my by-line on the first article. Now I understood why Christie had told us to bring our notebooks from the Against Taffy Sinclair Club. We had recorded every snotty thing Taffy did during the entire fifth grade. And I could remember a lot of things she'd done this year, too.

"Christie, you're a genius," I said. "We've probably got enough material in our notebooks to write a dozen exposés."

"Maybe even a book!" said Beth.

Suddenly all my best friends were thumbing

through their notebooks. Even Katie was getting into the act. She's usually above this sort of thing, but after all, she's our friend, not Taffy Sinclair's. "Here's one," she shouted. "'October fifteenth. Taffy Sinclair drops her lunch ticket in the cafeteria line. She is wearing a really short dress, and she bends over to pick up her ticket so that she can show her underpants.'"

We all started yelling and clapping like crazy. I was glad Christie's mother wasn't home. She would think we had gone berserk.

"I've got one," I offered.

"No, me! Me!" insisted Beth. "We've got to put this one in the exposé because of Mr. Scott. 'November ninth. Taffy Sinclair walks past Mr. Neal after the last bell rings. She puts her hand on her hip so her elbow will stick out and then she *brushes against his sleeve as she walks by!*'"

I could hear everybody yelling and clapping again, but I sat there feeling slightly numb. I remembered that day. I would never forget dreamy Mr. Neal, our fifth-grade teacher, and the huge crush I had on him. In fact, even thinking about him now made me feel all tingly. But most of all, I remembered Taffy Sinclair brushing against his sleeve and then looking straight at me. I'd get her for that. I'd write the greatest exposé that had ever been written.

For the next half hour we all went through our

notebooks calling out every truly mean and horrible thing she had done during fifth grade. After that we remembered everything she had done so far this year. As my friends would think of something new I'd write it down on a blank sheet in my notebook.

"Jana, remember when she tried to teach you body language and she said yours looked like baby talk?" asked Christie. I shot her a poison-dart look. I certainly wasn't going to print a thing like that.

Still, the more things we thought of, the happier I was that Christie had come up with the idea of writing an exposé of Taffy Sinclair.

## 9 ✣

When I got home, Mom still wasn't there, even though it was time for her to be getting off work. I was glad I had beaten her home. She might start asking a lot of questions if she saw my Against Taffy Sinclair Club notebook. This way I could sneak it back into my room and even begin working on the exposé. I could hardly wait to get started.

I plopped the notebook on my desk. Then I looked in my mirror. I couldn't resist. And there was my twin. In all the excitement over writing an exposé of Taffy Sinclair, I had almost forgotten about her. I stopped and looked at her. She looked back at me.

I sat down at my desk and got out a clean sheet of paper. This was going to be great. I was really going to get back at Taffy Sinclair. I stared at that clean sheet of paper. Getting the first sentence down would be the hardest. After that it would be a cinch. I glanced out of the corner of my eye to see if my twin was watching me. She was, out of the corner of her eye. I sighed. It was really hard to write something important with another person looking over your shoulder.

A little while later the front door slammed. It was Mom. I grabbed the notebook, stuffed it under the bed, and opened my social studies book just as she barged into my room.

"I suppose there's some good reason why you haven't started dinner," she said sarcastically.

"I didn't know you wanted me to," I said.

"Then apparently you neglected to read my note."

My ears started to get hot. I hadn't seen any note. We always left notes for each other on the fridge, but I hadn't noticed her note to me when I put mine up to tell her I was going to Christie's. I hadn't noticed it when I got home and took mine down, either. Actually I hadn't paid any attention. I had had too many things on my mind.

I thought fast. "Gosh, Mom. I guess I was just too preoccupied with this fascinating report we have to write for social studies," I lied.

Mom rolled her eyes and gazed toward the ceiling as if she expected to find the answers to all her problems written there. "What fascinating report is that?"

Frantically I looked around my room for an idea and saw my mirror. "Twins," I blurted out. "We have to write a report on twins, and gosh, are they fascinating. Wiggins even read us an article out of a magazine about twins who got separated when they were really little. Do you know anything about twins?"

The minute those words were out of my mouth, I thought I'd die. I hadn't *meant* to say a thing like that. Mom had a funny look on her face. She was probably thinking about my twin and wishing she were here right now.

"What do I know about twins?" she asked almost dreamily. "Pink is a twin." She was staring off into the distance as if she were in some sort of trance, and I could swear that her eyes were filling up with tears. My heart started to pound. What would I do if she started to cry? Then all of a sudden she came to life and shrugged. "Twins? What do I know about anything? I thought I knew some things. I thought I knew about Wallace Pinkerton. Boy, what a fool I was. Now, come on into the kitchen and help me get supper. I've had a terrible day. I'm exhausted and I don't intend to do everything myself. You're going to have to help."

It was my turn to be practically in a trance. I did have a twin. I was sure of it now. Mom had looked so far away. She'd almost *cried*. She wouldn't do that just because Pink was a twin. Why would that make her sad?

I had a twin, all right. The clues were everywhere. First there were the pictures and Mom's flimsy excuse that they were both me and that they had to be taken separately. Then there was the other little girl in the kiddie pool the day I stepped on the bee.

I closed my eyes and concentrated really hard, trying to remember everything I could about that day. Finally I started to see her face. It was getting clearer and clearer, as if she were stepping out of a fog. She had long dark hair just like mine and blue eyes just like mine. I knew it. She was the other little girl in the picture!

"Jana!" bellowed Mom from the kitchen. "Are you coming or not?"

"Yeah, Mom. I'll be right there."

I sighed. I hated it when she was crabby like this. It was bad enough that my father acted as if I didn't exist and spent all his time with my twin. But when Mom was in one of her moods, she didn't know I existed either. It was as if I were all alone in the world. I looked at my twin. I couldn't help wishing I could talk to her through the mirror.

I'd ask her about my father, I thought. I bet he's a whole lot easier to live with than Mom is. I bet he's never crabby, or if he is, he doesn't take things out on her. After all, it's not my fault Mom and Pink aren't getting along. I couldn't help envying my twin just a little for having it so much better than I did. I thought about that for a minute. What if my father has a lot of money and they live in a mansion with a swimming pool? What if he takes her to Europe and Hollywood all the time and introduces her to movie stars? Or rock stars? What if she has a horse! I wondered what it would be like to trade places with her for a while.

Mom didn't say much while we fixed hamburgers and french fries for supper. She didn't say much while we ate, either, except once when the phone rang.

"Jana, get that, will you?" she said. "And if it's Wallace Pinkerton, tell him I'm not in."

I thought about all the times she told me never to lie and say I'm not in when it was someone I didn't want to talk to, but I kept my mouth shut. Thank goodness it was a wrong number.

After the dishes were done, I went back to my room to work on my exposé of Taffy Sinclair. I sighed and stared at the blank sheet of paper some more. I tried to feel as mad at Taffy as I had felt that afternoon. The only problem was, I couldn't.

It wasn't that I had suddenly started to like Taffy Sinclair. It was just that I couldn't help thinking about my twin and how lucky she was.

Then I got this great idea. What if I told my father that I knew about my twin? Maybe he would let her come for a visit sometime. Maybe he would even let me trade places with her for a little while.

The more I thought about my great idea, the better it sounded. It was only Wednesday night. The *Sentinel* deadline wasn't until Friday, so I didn't have to work on my exposé until tomorrow night. Getting even with Taffy was important, but finding out about my twin could change my life. The problem was, how was I going to do it?

I sat there thinking for quite a while, and when the answer came to me, it was so simple that I didn't know why I hadn't thought of it before. I remembered how Cynthia on *Interns and Lovers* had tried and tried to contact her father all these years just the same way I had. It hadn't worked for her and it hadn't worked for me. But when Cynthia wrote a deathbed letter, she got results. Even though I wasn't on my deathbed, I decided to try the same tactic. I was sure my father would forgive me as soon as he realized how important it was for me to know about my twin.

I took out a sheet of stationery. *Dear Father,* I

wrote. I tried to make my handwriting a little bit squiggly so he would think I was almost too weak to hold my pen.

*I am writing this letter from my deathbed....*

# 10 ✻

*O*n the way to school the next morning I wondered if it was still too soon to tell my friends about my twin. I was dying to see how they would take the news. Would they be jealous? After all, having an identical twin was a pretty big thing, especially since everybody thought I was an only child. Even Taffy Sinclair couldn't top a thing like that.

I dropped the letter to my father into the corner mailbox, thinking that I should probably wait until I knew more about my twin before I said anything. I knew my friends would ask a million questions. I could see it all now. As soon as the word got out, kids would crowd around me. They would have so many questions that I would have to ask them to raise their hands. Then I would point to the kid whose question I wanted to answer next just like the President does when he has a news conference. Right now I wasn't ready for that.

Which was just as well, because nobody paid the slightest bit of attention to me when I got to school. At first I didn't even see my friends. Then I noticed a group of ten or twelve girls over by the bicycle racks. They were all talking excitedly, and right in the middle were my best friends. I couldn't help feeling a little bit funny since I had just been imagining everyone crowded around *me*. I wondered what was going on. I couldn't tell until I heard somebody say, "Gosh, Melanie. You look great. How much weight have you lost?"

There in the middle of that crowd stood Melanie, and I have to admit she did look great. She had on new designer jeans that must have been at least two sizes smaller than her usual size, and a gorgeous white blouse with lace panels up each sleeve. You could tell she was really pleased with herself, too, from the grin on her face.

"As of this morning, twelve pounds and counting," she said with a little laugh.

Twelve pounds and counting, I thought grimly. She might look good now, but before she knew it, she would be just skin and bones, a tiny frail bird.

I sighed. I was the only one who knew the truth: Melanie was anorexic. I would have to go into action to save her.

I ducked around the corner of the building, dashed in the side door and skidded to a stop at the candy machine. I dug into my jeans pocket and came up with three quarters, two dimes, and two nickels. It was every cent I owned, but it would buy three candy bars. I didn't know if that would be enough to save Melanie, but I had to try.

"Don't you know that all that candy will give you cavities?"

My heart stopped. It was Randy Kirwan. I hadn't even heard him come up behind me. Now he probably thought I was a pig for buying so much candy. I was so embarrassed I thought I'd die.

By the time I looked up, he was already halfway down the hall, but he was looking back over his shoulder and smiling. I thought about running after him and explaining that they weren't really for me, but Radar Rollins rounded the corner, and I decided to stay where I was. Maybe I could explain things to Randy later. I closed my eyes, imagining.

"Oh, Randy," I would say. "I really appreciate your being concerned about my teeth, but the candy was for someone else."

"That's wonderful, Jana. It's just that I'm so

crazy about you that I couldn't stand to think of you in pain, getting your teeth filled."

Suddenly I opened my eyes. Why hadn't I thought of that before? Randy didn't think I was a pig. He just didn't want me to be in pain. Hadn't I noticed how much attention he was paying to me lately? Hadn't I been absolutely certain that he was beginning to be crazy about me? How much more proof did I need?

I felt as if everything had suddenly started going my way, and I had a hard time thinking about anything else all morning in class. Randy Kirwan had proved just how much he cared for me. I was probably going to save my friend Melanie from dying of anorexia. I was going to write an exposé of Taffy Sinclair so everyone would see her for what she really was. And I was going to find out all about my twin and maybe even trade places with her for a while.

I was still feeling pretty good when I got to the cafeteria for lunch. I was planning to sit next to Melanie and dump all three candy bars into her lunch bag when she wasn't looking. With her sweet tooth she'd never be able to resist. But she outmaneuvered me the moment I sat down, by jumping up and moving to the other side of the table between Christie and Beth.

"I think Scott Daly likes me," she said confidentially. "I want to sit over here where I can see him."

"Scott Daly?" asked Katie. She looked so surprised that she almost dropped her sandwich. "What makes you think he likes you?"

"He's been borrowing things all morning. First a pencil. Then paper—twice. He's never done that before. I think he noticed that I've lost weight."

"Gosh, maybe *I'll* go on a diet if it will make somebody as cute as Scott Daly notice me," said Christie, which was pretty funny, since she's the thinnest one of us all.

Melanie only giggled and took a teensy bite out of her apple.

"You really do look great," said Beth. "Why don't you try out for a part on a soap opera and give Taffy Sinclair a little competition?"

Melanie remained silent. You could tell she was thinking the idea over. Then she shook her head. "I wouldn't want to miss school three days every week. That would leave only two days for me to see Scott."

Good grief, I thought. All I need is for Melanie to get a boyfriend. I'd never be able to save her. I hadn't been able to slip the candy bars into her lunch bag, but I decided it wouldn't have done any good anyway, since she was so busy watching Scott Daly that she didn't touch her hard-boiled egg and just nibbled on her apple. Of course, I wouldn't let the candy bars go to waste while I thought up another way to save her.

Christie asked me to come to her house to watch *Interns and Lovers* after school, but I made the excuse that I had to get home because Mom had left me a long list of jobs to do, and after that I had to work on my exposé of Taffy Sinclair. Actually I just wanted to be by myself when Cynthia started talking about her twin again. I might even want to take notes.

As soon as the show came on, I was sorry I hadn't gone to Christie's. In the very first scene Taffy Sinclair was sitting up in bed with about a half dozen doctors and nurses looking down at her. Poor Cynthia wasn't even in sight. This time Taffy had on a lavender nightgown with a white lace collar. Also, it looked like she was wearing false eyelashes and she had the most icky sweet grin on her face that I had ever seen.

*"Thank you all for coming to my room,"* she said in a fake southern accent. I couldn't believe my ears. Not only was she saying lines, but she was using the most *horrible* fake southern accent in the world. *"And thank you all especially for takin' such good care of me."*

I couldn't listen. I covered my ears with my hands, but I could still see her on the screen, grinning her icky sweet grin and batting her eyelashes and talking in her accent. It was so awful I thought I'd die.

I stood it as long as I could. Then I jumped up and raced to my room. I didn't even care if I missed seeing Cynthia. I sat down at my desk and grabbed a sheet of notebook paper and a pencil. Across the top I wrote: THE TRUTH ABOUT TAFFY SINCLAIR. Everything that she had ever done came pouring out of my mind and onto that paper. I must have scribbled as hard as I could for twenty minutes. When I was finished, I was panting as if I had just run a race, but I knew I had written a super exposé. Now everybody would see Taffy Sinclair for what she really was.

I could hear the television going in the living room. I had been in such a hurry that I hadn't even turned it off. I looked at my watch. *To Have and to Hold* would just be coming on. What was happening in poor Samantha's life? Was Michael still sneaking around with Terri? I went into the living room and switched the channel. There was Samantha and Michael, and it looked as if they were having a very serious talk.

*"Samantha, honey, what do I have to do to convince you that there is nothing going on between Terri and me? I'm just nice to her because she's your best friend."*

*"I really want to believe you, Michael. It's just that—"* Michael took her in his arms before she could

say any more and kissed her. The rat! You could tell Samantha wanted to believe him.

*"Then do believe me. You're making a big deal over nothing. Terri doesn't mean a thing to me."*

They kissed again. Samantha was really convinced now. How could she be so stupid? The commercials came on, and I went to the kitchen for a can of soda. When I got back, Michael was in his sports car driving along a moonlit beach road. I knew where he was going—for another rendezvous with Terri on the beach! Sure enough, he parked his car and started walking toward the water. An instant later Terri stepped out of the shadows. They ran toward each other as the show ended for the day.

I turned off the television. I had had enough for one day. Still, I couldn't get Samantha out of my mind. She was so crazy about Michael that she would believe anything he said. I felt sorry for her. It was obvious that she was going to get hurt.

I was still sitting on the sofa with my empty soda can when Mom came home. "Hi, love," she chirped as she took off her coat and hung it in the hall closet. "How was your day?"

Mom was actually in a good mood. I couldn't believe it. "Fine," I said. "How was yours?"

"Great!" Mom went into the kitchen, and I could hear her humming as she started supper. Minutes went by, and she didn't even yell at me to come in and help. I was beginning to think she had come down with something when I smelled it—Mom's homemade spaghetti sauce! Every summer she freezes some and saves it for special occasions. She calls those occasions Celebration Suppers.

"Yahoo!" I shouted as I hopped into the kitchen and grabbed a spoon for a quick taste. "Celebration Supper! What happened? Did you get a raise?"

"Better than that," she said. She put her arms around me and gave me a big hug. Grinning, she got out these special tongs and began pulling spaghetti out of the colander and piling it onto our plates. My mouth was watering like crazy. "I'm sorry I've been in such a bad mood lately," she went on. "I shouldn't have taken my problems with Pink out on you."

"That's okay, Mom," I said, feeling a little guilty about some of the thoughts I'd had. I looked down quickly, watching her ladle sauce onto the spaghetti as if it were the most fascinating event of my life. For a reason I couldn't explain, I was also feeling a little suspicious.

"Well, everything is going to be okay from now on." Mom paused a minute, looking thoughtful. Then she motioned for me to sit down at the table. "I was disturbed because I thought Pink was paying too much attention to a woman at the bowling alley. Thank goodness I finally decided to talk to him about it. And do you know what? He convinced me that I was making a big deal over nothing!"

*A big deal over nothing.* Those words were ringing in my ears. Now I understood why I was feeling suspicious. That was the same thing Michael told Samantha, and she believed him, too.

# 11 *

*F*riday afternoon, after I left my exposé of Taffy Sinclair in Mr. Cagney's box in the office, I ducked out on my friends and hurried home to watch my soaps in private. Taffy had been in school so I knew she wouldn't be on *Interns and Lovers*. I was glad, because I was desperate to know more about Cynthia and her twin. What would happen next? Would they get together? Also, for Melanie's sake, I needed to know if Cynthia was still getting worse or if she had finally decided to eat. And Chad. I hadn't seen him in two whole days.

I turned on the set and settled down on the sofa, thinking about how familiar the show's theme music was beginning to sound. That wasn't all that

80

was familiar. I had only been watching one week, and already I knew more about the people on it and their problems than I did about anyone else in the whole world, even my best friends. It was as if they had all told me their secrets. The exception was Taffy Sinclair. I didn't feel close to her at all. She was just a fake. But the others weren't fakes. Not Cynthia. Not Chad. Not even Cynthia's twin.

Samantha and Michael weren't fakes either, and they were helping me to understand about Mom and Pink. Pink had certainly fooled me as much as he had fooled Mom. But now I knew what kind of jerk he was and that he would break Mom's heart if I didn't find some way to stop him.

When the commercials finally ended and the opening scene of *Interns and Lovers* came on the screen, there was a young woman sitting on a sofa reading a book. She had dark hair just like Cynthia's. In fact, she looked exactly like Cynthia except she didn't have dark circles under her eyes and her cheeks weren't sunken in. I knew who she was—Cynthia's twin.

I was staring at her so hard and my heart was pounding so loudly that I almost didn't notice when a man entered the room and began speaking.

*"Stephanie, may I interrupt your reading, dear? There is something that I really must talk to you about."*

Stephanie. Cynthia's twin was named Stephanie!

I moved to the floor right in front of the television set and turned the volume up so that I wouldn't miss a thing.

"*Sure, Dad. What is it?*"

The man was holding a piece of paper in his hand. Cynthia's letter, I thought. He sat down beside Stephanie on the sofa. You could tell by the serious look on his face that he was carefully thinking over what he was going to say. "*Stephanie, dear, in a city not far from here is someone I must tell you about. For many years I have thought it best to keep her existence a secret from you, but I now know that has been a mistake.*"

Stephanie looked puzzled, but she didn't say anything. Her father had stopped talking, too. I was getting really antsy. "Go ahead and tell her," I muttered.

He looked her straight in the eye, but still he didn't speak. I was about to go berserk when finally he said, "*Stephanie, you have an identical twin sister.*"

"*What?*" she gasped. "*An identical twin sister? I don't understand. What are you talking about?*"

Then her father told her all about the divorce and how he and her mother had each decided to keep a twin and not tell her about the other one.

"*At the time we thought it was the right thing to do,*" he said. "*But a few days ago I received this letter from your sister and learned that she is gravely ill. In fact, she's going to die. So this morning I wrote to her and told her about you."*

He had tears in his eyes as he handed Cynthia's letter to Stephanie to read. When she looked up again, she had tears in her eyes, too, and I felt a lump the size of a tennis ball form in my throat.

*"I have a twin, and her name is Cynthia,"* she said as if she couldn't believe the words herself. She jumped to her feet. *"I must go to her,"* she said. *"I must leave right now and go to her bedside to be with her when she dies!"*

I was crying so hard that I could hardly see the television screen, but it didn't matter because the program was over for the day. All I could think about was Stephanie and how glad she was to know she had a twin. She was even going to go to her and be with her when she died.

I thought about my own twin and the letter I had written to my father. Would he tell her about me the way Stephanie's father had told her about Cynthia? How would she feel? Would she want to be with me when I died? The thought made me shivery, especially since my letter had been a teensy little lie. Still, it would all be worth it if I got to see my twin.

That night I had a dream. It was about Mom and Pink. They were on lane six at the bowling alley. I was there, too, but I wasn't bowling. I was just sort of hanging around, and they didn't even see me.

Mom looked really happy. She kept smiling up at Pink. I had to admit that he was treating her pretty nicely, smiling back at her and applauding every time she knocked down some pins. I was beginning to think I had been wrong about him, until I noticed how he kept glancing toward the snack bar whenever Mom was taking her turn.

I also noticed that there was a girl working in the snack bar and *she* kept glancing toward lane six. She looked familiar, so I sneaked over in that direction for a better view. I couldn't believe my eyes. It was Terri from *To Have and to Hold*!

I woke up with a start. I could still see Pink and Terri gazing at each other across the crowded bowling alley, and Mom, poor Mom, taking her turn at bowling as if nothing in the world were wrong. I knew I had to do something. I had to save her from a broken heart. But how? I lay there in the dark for a long time, trying to think up something to do. What would Samantha do? I wondered. But Samantha wouldn't be any help now. This weekend Mom and Pink would go bowling like they always do, and the soaps wouldn't be on again until Monday. By then it would be too late.

Then I got this great idea. I would do just what

I had done in my dream. I would spy on Pink at the bowling alley! I could call one of my friends, probably Beth, and see if I could spend the night. Then we would talk her parents into dropping us off for an evening of bowling. At the bowling alley I could watch Pink and catch him red-handed, cheating on Mom.

My plan worked like a charm. I told Beth about it the next day, and she thought it was a great idea; but then I knew she would, since she likes to be dramatic. She talked to her parents, and they said they would pick me up at my apartment at 7:30 and take us straight to the bowling alley. The bad thing was that I was still home when Pink came to pick up Mom. Of course, she yelled to me to answer the door.

"Hi there, Jana," Pink said. He had just about the biggest grin I'd ever seen plastered all over his face. "It's good to see you. How've you been?"

"Fine," I mumbled as he pushed a warm pizza box into my arms. Pink always brings me a pizza when he takes Mom out for the evening. I had to admit that the pizza smelled heavenly.

Then Mom came into the room, and Pink's grin got even bigger, if that's possible.

"Hi, sweetheart. You look gorgeous tonight," he said, kissing her on the forehead. He turned to me again. "Doesn't she look especially gorgeous tonight, Jana?"

It was all I could do to keep from throwing up all over that heavenly-smelling pizza. Couldn't Mom see what a fake Pink was? That he was just like that cad Michael? But Mom was grinning back at him, and she did look especially pretty in her new beige and rust outfit.

After they left, I ate my pizza and waited for Beth, worrying about Mom and hoping, for her sake, that my plan would work. But as soon as we got to the bowling alley, I started to worry. It didn't look a thing like the one in my dream, and it was so noisy and crowded that we could barely move around.

"Let's look for the snack bar," I said, but Beth had already taken off in the direction of the lanes.

"We've got to find your mom and Pink first," she insisted. "If we don't know where they are, how are we going to keep out of their sight?"

I had to admit that what she said made a lot of sense.

"There they are," she shouted a minute later. "On lane six!"

I couldn't believe it, but there they were on lane six, just like in my dream! Deep down I knew that my dream had been a premonition and that coming to the bowling alley to spy on Pink had been the right thing to do.

Beth and I found seats behind two really big men in the observation section. We could peek around the men to watch Mom and Pink, and duck back behind them whenever we thought we might be seen. It worked pretty well, but it got to be deadly dull.

"First your mom gets up and bowls and Pink grins at her like it was a big deal. Then Pink gets up and bowls and your mom grins at him. Then your mom gets up to bowl..." Beth said. "Terminal boredom! When is Pink going to do something?"

I was wondering the same thing when I saw Pink say something to Mom and walk up the stairs away from the lane.

"There he goes!" I shouted. Thank goodness he was too far away and the place was too noisy for him to hear me. "Let's follow him and see what he's really up to. I'll bet he's heading for a rendezvous."

Slowly and carefully Beth sneaked out of her seat and slipped into the crowd. I was right behind her. Pink had been heading toward the back of the bowling alley. That must be where the snack bar was, I thought. The snack bar and his rendezvous.

Beth stopped for a minute to let a woman carrying a tray of drinks pass in front of her. "Rats!" she said over her shoulder. "Now I've lost him."

"Let's split up and look for him," I suggested. "We can meet again by the front door."

"Good idea," said Beth. "In fifteen minutes my parents are going to pick us up anyway."

Fifteen minutes. That wasn't much time. I charged through the crowd, more determined than ever. It was now or never.

Just then I spotted him again. I could see Pink's blond head above all the other heads in front of me. I slithered through the crowd, saying "Excuse me" every time I bumped somebody or stepped on a toe. I had almost reached him when a door opened and Pink disappeared inside. I've got him now, I thought triumphantly. Suddenly I was standing in front of that door. I couldn't believe my eyes. Right in the middle it said MEN.

I headed for the front door of the bowling alley feeling really depressed. Had Pink spotted me and figured out that I was tailing him? Had he ducked into the men's room to get away? I was sure he had, and I left the bowling alley thinking that Beth and I would have to come up with a better plan before Pink took Mom bowling again next Saturday night.

# 12 *

If I had known ahead of time what Monday morning would bring, I would have spent my weekend packing and getting out of town instead of spying on Pink and moping around about my twin. I would have headed for the Himalayas or stowed away aboard a freighter bound for Australia. I certainly wouldn't have gone to school and walked right into trouble.

My first warning came from Christie. She was waiting for me when I got to the school grounds, and she had a scared look on her face. My three other friends were with her, and they all looked scared, too.

"Jana, have you lost your mind?" she shrieked.

"Yeah, Jana. What's the big idea?" demanded

Beth. "Didn't you know you'd get us all in trouble?"

"Would somebody please tell me what's going on?" I asked. I couldn't figure out what was the matter with them.

"You tell her, Christie," said Melanie. "You're the one who saw it."

"Saw what?" I insisted.

"The *Mark Twain Sentinel,* that's what," said Christie. "When Beth and I got to school this morning, we just happened to stop in the office for a minute—"

"She was trying to catch a glimpse of Mr. Scott," interrupted Beth.

Christie shot her a poison-dart look. "*And* the *Sentinel* was there on the desk, ready to be handed out during first period. Anyway, on the *front* page is your exposé of Taffy Sinclair, and instead of Curtis Trowbridge's by-line, it has *yours!*"

"*Mine!*" This time I was shrieking. "That's impossible! When I put it in Mr. Cagney's box it said 'by Curtis Trowbridge.' I swear it did. Nobody was ever supposed to know I wrote it."

"Well, whoever types up the stories for Mr. Cagney must have figured it out, since Curtis is out of town, and switched by-lines. After all, the first article about Taffy Sinclair had your by-line on it," said Katie. "What did you put into that story, anyway? Is there a lot of stuff about us?"

I didn't answer for a minute. I was wracking my

brain, trying to remember. "Well, I put in how she used to flirt with Mr. Neal in fifth grade. I thought Mr. Scott ought to know a thing like that." I was sure that would make Christie feel better, but when I looked at her, her scared expression hadn't changed. "And I put in how she uses body language to send messages to cute boys. And how conceited she is and how she brags to everybody all the time. I put in lots of stuff like that, but I didn't use any of our names," I said.

Suddenly I felt a jab in my ribs. It was Melanie, and she looked even more scared than before. "Don't look now," she whispered hoarsely, "but guess who *didn't* go into New York City for filming today and who *did* come to school?"

Taffy Sinclair. I couldn't help looking. She was here, and she was going to read that exposé along with everybody else.

Mr. Scott distributed the paper first thing that morning. Everybody was pretty quiet as they looked it over. I held my breath, and then I heard Taffy gasp.

"What!" She stood up and started screaming her head off. "'The Truth About Taffy Sinclair'! Jana Morgan, how could you! How could you write such terrible lies?"

The rest of the class was snickering and giggling and making crazy faces at each other. Everybody except me. I just sat in my seat, poker-stiff, looking down at my paper as if nothing unusual was going on at all. But I was cringing. I was cringing so hard I was probably shrinking.

Just then the intercom speaker crackled on, and I could hear Miss Graves, the office secretary, clearing her throat. "Will Jana Morgan report to the office at once," she said. "I repeat, Jana Morgan report to the office at once."

I was doomed. I knew that my life was over. I would probably be expelled. And the school would probably call my mother and tell her everything. I got up and shuffled out of the room with all eyes on me, thinking that it was Christie who should be expelled. Writing that exposé had been her idea in the first place. But deep down I knew that I was the one who had actually written it, and that it had been a rotten thing to do.

"Sit down, Jana," said Mr. Scott when I got to the office. I was sorry that it was Mr. Scott I had to see instead of Mrs. Winchell, Christie's mother. She might have been easy on me since I'm Christie's friend. Not only that, but it had been because Mr. Scott was tutoring Taffy that I had written the article in the first place.

The minute I sat down, he stood up. I hadn't realized how tall he was. He was so tall it looked as if his head were touching the ceiling, and he was glaring down at me angrily.

"First let me say that if Mr. Cagney had not

been ill with the flu this weekend and had not okayed all the stories for publication without reading them as he usually does, your article about Taffy Sinclair would never have been printed."

Boy, did I wish Mr. Cagney had never gotten the flu. I wished he felt so wonderful he had read all the articles three times.

"But Mr. Cagney did get sick, and the article did get printed, and unfortunately no faculty member happened to read the paper before it was handed out first period," Mr. Scott continued. "And I can only say that I am both shocked and disappointed that you would be so jealous of your classmate that you would write such a thing."

Jealous! How could Mr. Scott think a thing like that? It was all I could do to keep from jumping up and telling him that I could never be jealous of Taffy Sinclair. She was a terrible person. What's more, she was a fake, and I had written my article so that everybody, especially Mr. Scott, could see her for what she really was. But I just sat there and stared at the floor. It wouldn't do any good to tell him, anyway. It was plain to see he was taken in by Taffy Sinclair, too.

"There is nothing we can do to correct the damage that has been done," he went on. "But I must insist that you not write any more stories for the *Mark Twain Sentinel*. If you give me that promise, you may go back to your class."

"Yes, Mr. Scott. I promise," I muttered without looking at him. As I left his office I kept reminding myself that at least he hadn't expelled me from school or called my mother. How could I have let myself get talked into writing such an article? I wondered. I should have known that letting other people see you for what you really are is a lot different than trying to get them to see the truth about someone else. I was so embarrassed I thought I'd die.

Just as I got into the hall, I had the feeling that someone was staring at me. I looked up, and there was Randy Kirwan coming toward me carrying the attendance report to the office. It was his eyes I had felt. He was looking straight at me.

"Hi, Randy," I said when he got close enough to hear. My heart stopped. He didn't answer. He didn't say one word. He just got a funny look on his face and walked on by.

I had lost Randy Kirwan. I couldn't think of anything else the rest of the day. I had blown it with that exposé of Taffy Sinclair. So what if everybody knew that Taffy was mean and snotty and a fake if Randy thought I was really the one who was the villain?

# 13 ✳

*I* was so depressed that I didn't even want to watch the soaps when I got home. Instead, I threw myself across my bed facedown. My life was in just about the biggest mess imaginable. If ever there was a time to trade places with my twin, surely this was it. I closed my eyes and saw her as clearly as could be. This time she was all the way out of the fog and splashing and playing with me in the kiddie pool. *She* didn't think I was a villain. She liked me. I tried and tried to remember something else about her. What other things had we done together? But my memory started to get foggy again, and I felt even lonelier than before.

I thought of Julie on *To Live, Perchance to Love* and how much we had in common. Julie couldn't remember the hit-and-run accident or that she was married to Arthur. My heart began to pound as I raced for the television set and turned it on. I hadn't watched that show for days, and yet Julie was the one person in the world who would understand the way I felt when I couldn't remember my twin.

I had been lying across my bed longer than I thought. *To Live, Perchance to Love* was almost over, but Julie was there, just as I had hoped she would be. She was sitting at a kitchen table sipping coffee and talking to an older woman.

*"Mother, it's so frightening not being able to remember things. It's like being all alone in the world."*

I gulped hard and brushed away a tear that was starting to roll down my cheek. Boy, you can say that again, I thought. Julie's mother reached across the table and patted her hand.

*"I know, dear. But you must keep trying. Poor Arthur. He desperately needs for you to remember that you love him and are married to him, and of course, that he had nothing to do with the accident."*

*"I'm trying, Mother. I really am. Sometimes I close my eyes and try to see Arthur and me together. I almost can, except..."*

*"Except what, dear?"*

*"It's like... like looking through a fog. I can't quite see his face because of the fog."*

Fog! My heart swelled along with the organ

music as the show ended. When I had first remembered my twin, it had seemed as if she were coming out of the fog. Now Julie was looking into the same kind of fog trying to remember Arthur. I was right. I really was remembering my twin. Julie had just proved it. I almost wished Julie was my twin since we had so much in common. At the very least I wished the show weren't over for the day. I could hardly wait to see if Arthur's face would come all the way out of the fog.

Taffy wasn't at school the next day. I was glad. I wasn't ready to face the consequences of the article yet, even though hardly anybody said anything about it. Most kids had forgotten already, except for Mona Vaughn. She stuck her tongue out at me in the lunch line. But Taffy wasn't on *Interns and Lovers,* either. The episode was all about Stephanie getting ready to go see Cynthia. She was packing and making arrangements. The show ended as she was getting on a plane.

I knew that I should watch *To Have and to Hold* for Mom's sake, but I just couldn't. Not today. I was too antsy to sit still. So I paced the floor, waiting for *To Live, Perchance to Love* to come on, thinking about poor Julie and whether or not Arthur would come out of the fog. But when the show finally started, Julie wasn't on it. The whole episode was about that awful Dierdre and how she was plotting to have Arthur convicted of the hit-

and-run accident. Even though I felt sorry for Arthur, I couldn't help being disappointed. I would have to wait another whole day to see Julie.

The next morning Taffy still wasn't in school. I couldn't believe it. I was beginning to worry. Did her absence have anything to do with my exposé? I couldn't help mentioning her when my friends and I met in the cafeteria for lunch.

"I wonder where Taffy Sinclair has been lately?" I said. I tried to act casual so they wouldn't notice that I was beginning to feel nervous. "She wasn't at school yesterday, and she wasn't on the show either."

"Isn't it exciting about Cynthia's twin going to see her?" said Melanie. "I cried and cried, and I just know I'm going to cry again when they meet for the first time."

"Yeah, but what about Taffy?" I insisted. I hated it when people changed the subject without answering the question.

"She's probably sick," said Katie. "There's a lot of flu going around, you know."

You're telling me, I thought.

"Maybe she went into the city yesterday, and it was the wrong day," suggested Beth. "Maybe she wasn't supposed to be on the show until today."

I decided she was probably right, but when I got home from school and turned on *Interns and Lovers,* Taffy was nowhere to be seen. This time the show was all about Cynthia getting ready for her visit from Stephanie. She was telling Chad and the doctors and nurses how excited she was. You would have thought she'd have told Taffy Sinclair, too, since they were in the same room. But I watched the whole show, and never once did the camera swing around to Taffy's bed.

Now I was really worried. I was so worried that I hardly even paid attention to *To Live, Perchance to Love*, even though it was all about Dierdre again. If Arthur didn't come out of the fog for a few days, nothing bad would happen.

But where was Taffy Sinclair? I couldn't sleep all night. The next morning when I saw my friends, I could tell that they were worried, too.

"What's happened to her?" whispered Christie. She was looking around to make sure nobody except us heard what she was saying. "Do you suppose she ran away from home after she read the exposé?"

"Or something worse!" said Beth in her most dramatic voice.

"Like what?" I demanded.

Beth's eyes got really big. Then she ran her finger along her throat and made a slashing noise. "Maybe she couldn't face the fact that everybody knew the truth about her, so she ended it all," she said.

It was too horrible to think about. What if Beth was right? What if Taffy really had ended it all? It would be my fault. It would be because of my exposé. I was more depressed than ever now. And more worried. I might even go to jail if Taffy did something terrible because of the article I wrote.

When the bell rang, I went to our classroom. I was so worried about Taffy Sinclair that I was practically in a trance. About a half an hour later someone handed me a note. It was from Beth:

*Jana—*
*Meet me in the girls' bathroom before lunch. I have to show you what I found. It's awful!*

                                                        *Beth*

# 14 *

*I* didn't think the morning would ever end. I was beginning to wonder if I would grow old and die sitting at my desk. But finally it was lunchtime, and I made a mad dash for the girls' bathroom.

My four best friends and I got there at practically the same time. Beth went into her mysterious routine, holding up her hand for quiet and checking all the stalls to make sure no one was listening. Finally she decided we were safe.

"Here. Look what I found." She held out a folded-up piece of paper. It was obviously a note and didn't look special. In fact, it looked just like the notes everybody passes all the time. Just the same, Beth's hand was shaking.

"I found it lying beside Taffy Sinclair's locker, and it's in her handwriting."

Beth pushed it toward me as if it were a poisonous snake. I didn't want to take it. I was afraid of what I'd find inside, but I had to know. I opened it up and read it. I couldn't believe my eyes.

*I can't go on any longer. It's just too painful to*

The note ended there. I stared at it for a minute and then passed it to my friends. It was Taffy's squiggly handwriting, all right.

"It's just too painful to...what?" I whispered.

"I don't know," said Christie. "But whatever it was, it was so painful she couldn't even finish the note."

"I'm scared," said Melanie in a high-pitched voice. Two tears rolled down her cheeks.

"Me, too," said Katie.

"Me, too," I said. "But come on, let's go to the cafeteria. Lunch is half over already."

We scrambled out the door.

"I'm still scared," said Christie as we gathered at a corner table in the cafeteria.

Melanie looked as if she were about to cry again. "Me, too. What are we going to do?"

Nobody said anything. We just sat there passing that note around and thinking awful thoughts. My heart was pounding so hard it felt as if it were about to jump right out of my chest. I hadn't meant for anything like this to happen when I wrote that exposé. If only I could find Taffy and tell her that—before it was too late.

After school we promised to call one another if we heard anything. Beth gave me the note, and I sort of got the feeling that everybody thought I should be the one to do something about it. I suppose I couldn't blame them. It was my article and my by-line.

When I got home, I walked right past the television set and went to Mom's radio on the kitchen counter. She kept it set to the local station so that in the morning she could find out if bad weather was causing school closings or delays. I knew the local news came on every half hour and that if anything terrible had happened to Taffy Sinclair, I'd hear about it. Some dumb song was playing. Ten more minutes until the news.

I pulled Taffy's note out of my pocket and sat down at the kitchen table to wait. I read it over and over, trying to imagine what it meant. Suppose she was doing something terrible right this minute? Suppose she was on Bridgeport Beach near the spot where she and Mr. Scott had almost kissed? I closed my eyes. I could see it all. There was Taffy, standing alone, gazing out across the water. Tears were rolling down her cheeks, and this time they weren't fake. Now she was starting

to walk slowly out into the surf. I knew what she
was going to do. I had to stop her! Suddenly I was
tearing across the sand after her.

"Taffy! Stop! Don't do it! I'm sorry I wrote those
awful things!"

I came out of my daydream in time to hear the
radio announcer say, "And that's it for the three-
thirty news. Stay tuned. We'll be back at four."

I couldn't believe it. I had missed the news. That
made me feel even guiltier than ever. What was I
going to do? I could never get to Bridgeport
Beach and back before the four o'clock news.
Besides, she might be somewhere else. She might
even be at home. There were a lot of awful things
a person could do at home.

I knew I could call her to see if she was all right,
and if she was, I could tell her I was sorry. I stared
at the phone. I tried to stand up, but my knees
gave way and I heard a funny crackling sound in
my ears. Not only that, I felt as if I were going to
throw up.

Deep down I knew that I was really just a
coward. As much as I wanted to save Taffy, I
couldn't. I didn't have the nerve. I would probably
never be a hero in my whole life.

Then I got this great idea. I don't know why I
hadn't thought of it before. I needed a hero to
save Taffy Sinclair. Randy Kirwan was a hero. I
knew he would jump off a building to save an old

lady from being mugged if he had to. He was also kind and sensitive, and even though he thought I was a villain, I was sure he would try to save Taffy if he knew she was in trouble.

This time I didn't have any trouble standing up and going to the phone. I dialed his number and listened to it ring. His mother answered.

"Hello," she said.

"Hi. This is Jana Morgan. Is Randy home?"

"Oh, I'm sorry, Jana. Randy hasn't come home from football practice yet. He should be here in about half an hour. Can I have him call you?"

Half an hour. That might be too late.

"No, thanks, Mrs. Kirwan. That's okay."

I hung up the phone and headed out the door. I had another plan. If he was due home in half an hour, he was probably still at the school. So I would wait for him by the bicycle racks outside the gym.

My plan worked. I had just gotten to the school when I saw him come out of the gym with some other guys. I hadn't even stopped panting yet. Randy hesitated for a second when he saw me, and I had the awful feeling that he was going to duck back into the gym to avoid me, but thank goodness he didn't.

He must have known I wanted to talk to him because he left his friends and came over to me. He just stood there, waiting for me to say something.

I knew I had to do it and do it fast before I lost my nerve. I pulled Taffy's note out of my pocket and handed it to him as I started to talk.

"Taffy Sinclair hasn't been in school since...since the *Sentinel* came out, and she hasn't been on *Interns and Lovers,* either. My friends and I were starting to worry about her and then we found this note."

Randy read the note and frowned. I couldn't tell if he was frowning because he was worried about her or because he was mad at me.

"I know that I should go to her house or call her or something since I was the one who wrote that awful article, but..." I tried to gulp away the lump that was stuck in my throat. Randy was looking straight at me now, and this time I was sure his frown was meant for me. "...but I guess I'd have to say I'm scared."

"Look, Jana. I used to think you were a pretty nice person. But after all those terrible things you wrote about Taffy, I'm not sure anymore." He paused and looked at the note again. My heart felt as if someone were stabbing it with a knife. "I'll go to Taffy's house. Something might be wrong. But don't think of it as a favor to you."

Randy stuffed the note in his shirt pocket and jumped on his bike. He didn't say another word. He just took off down the street as fast as he could.

"Call me when you find out something," I shouted, but I couldn't tell whether he'd heard me.

I watched him ride away, knowing that I had lost him forever. He would never think I was a kind and sensitive person again.

All the way home I kept crossing and uncrossing my fingers and saying little prayers, hoping Taffy was all right. When I got to our apartment, I could hear the phone ringing inside. I dashed in and grabbed it. I tried to say hello, but only air came out of my mouth.

"Jana? Is that you?"

It was Mom. "Uh-huh," was all I could say.

"Where have you been? I've been calling for fifteen minutes. Never mind. Stay there. Don't leave for anything! I'm coming straight home and I've got something *very* important to talk to you about."

"Okay," I said. My hands were trembling when I hung up. Mom worked at the newspaper. They got news as fast as the radio station did. Sometimes even faster. Was she coming home to tell me something awful had happened to Taffy Sinclair?

# 15 ✾

*I* was pacing the floor like crazy when Mom walked
in the door, and I could tell by the look on her
face that she was upset. I held my breath while she
took off her coat, hung it up, came into the living
room and sat down on the sofa. I knew I was
supposed to sit down with her, so I did.

"Jana, I just got a call at work from your father,
and he's very upset. He said you wrote him a letter
and said you were dying."

I fell back against the sofa, letting out all the
breath I was holding. It wasn't bad news about
Taffy Sinclair after all. But as I remembered what
I had written in that letter to my father, a prickly
feeling went up my spine.

"You scared him half to death, Jana," Mom was

108

saying. "What on earth made you do a thing like that?"

I just looked at her for a minute. This was going to be hard to explain. "I was trying to get him to tell me about my secret identical twin."

"What do you mean, your secret identical twin?" Mom asked.

"Just like on *Interns and Lovers*," I said. "You see, Cynthia's parents were divorced when she was little, just like you and my father. Cynthia's father never came to see her, and he hardly ever wrote. Then, when she was dying of anorexia, she wrote him one last letter. He wrote back and told her that the reason he had not paid much attention to her all these years was because she had an identical twin sister who lived with him. And now Stephanie—that's her twin's name—is on her way to the hospital to be with Cynthia when she dies."

It was Mom's turn to sink back against the sofa. I could tell that she was really surprised, but she didn't look as if she were going to cry.

"Honey, *Interns and Lovers* is just a soap opera, a story. The people who write them try to make them as intriguing and exciting as they can so that viewers will get hooked and have to watch every day to see what will happen next. Besides, just because you and Cynthia both have fathers who ignore you doesn't mean the reasons are the same."

"But, Mom, just listen to this. Everything that

happens on those soaps comes true. First Cynthia quit eating and got anorexia. She told Chad it was because she wanted some self-control and discipline in her life. Now Melanie is losing weight like crazy, and she said the very same words."

I paused a minute to catch my breath, and Mom jumped in. She looked very stern.

"Jana, you are letting your imagination run away with you."

"No, I'm not. There's another thing. You know how you got mad at Pink for flirting with the woman at the bowling alley? Well, the same thing happened to Samantha on *To Have and to Hold*. Michael has been fooling around with her best friend, Terri. And you know how you had a talk with Pink and he told you it was no big deal? That's exactly what Michael told Samantha, and then he went to meet Terri again." I thought about telling her about my dream and how Beth and I had spied on her and Pink at the bowling alley, but I decided not to. Not now, anyway. Instead, I decided to drop the biggest bomb of all. "Besides, I know I have a secret twin. I can remember what she looks like. At first I couldn't, but then her face started coming out of the fog just like Arthur's on *To Live, Perchance to Love*. Besides, I have proof!"

I marched into my room and got my third-birthday picture out of my drawer. I looked at it for a minute. I had an awful feeling I knew what Mom would say.

But she didn't say a thing when I handed it to her. She didn't even mention that I had taped two pictures together. She just got a really sad look on her face and took me in her arms and held me.

"I'm sorry, Jana. I know how badly you've always wanted a brother or a sister, but you have to accept the fact that you do not have a twin. Sometimes when someone wants something as badly as you want a twin, she can make herself believe it's true."

"But Mom..." I insisted.

"There are two things I want you to see," she said. She took her arms from around me and got up, going into her bedroom. She was gone such a long time that I began to feel scared. I couldn't imagine what she wanted me to look at. Finally she came back and sat down beside me again. She had an old yellowed envelope in one hand and a small velvet box in the other.

"First the good news," she said with a nervous laugh. "Remember that silly grin Pink was wearing last Saturday night when he came to pick me up?"

I nodded. How could I forget a fake grin like that?

"Well, he kept grinning all evening while we bowled and then...when he brought me home, he gave me this." She opened the velvet box, and a gold ring with a small diamond in the middle winked up at me. My mouth dropped open. I couldn't believe my eyes. "He asked me to marry him," Mom said quietly. "So now you and I know that the woman at the bowling alley meant nothing to him. Thank you for caring, Jana, but Pink is not Michael, and I am not Samantha."

All I could do was look at Mom and then at the diamond and then at Mom again. "Why aren't you wearing it?" I burst out.

"Well," she said, "to be perfectly honest, I'm not sure I want to change our lives right now. And most of all, I wanted to talk it over with you before I made a decision, but I've been too much of a coward to mention it to you."

Mom and I both laughed, and she hugged me so tightly that the yellowed envelope slipped off her lap onto the floor. When she saw that, she stopped laughing and grew serious again.

"We've got lots of time to talk about whether Pink and I will get married," she said, and I felt relieved. "Now I want you to see this."

She picked up the envelope and handed it to me. I knew it had to have something to do with my twin. My hands were shaking as I opened it.

"My *birth* certificate!" I cried. I was so disappointed I thought I'd die. What did my birth certificate have to do with my twin? Besides, I had seen it a hundred times.

Mom pointed to a space on the paper that I hadn't noticed before. It was section 5A, and in tiny letters at the top of the space was printed *Plurality of birth* and beneath that was printed *Single* ☒ *Twin* ☐ *Triplet* ☐ *Other* ☐.

I sat and stared at that *X* in the square by *Single,* thinking that it didn't matter anymore if Cynthia and Stephanie got together or if Arthur's face came out of the fog. The little girl in the kiddie pool was not my twin, and she never had been.

"There *is* a reason why your father never comes to see you and seldom writes," Mom said after a while. "And I suppose you really do have a right to know what it is."

I looked at her in surprise. If it wasn't because of a twin, I couldn't imagine what it could be.

"You father has a problem, honey. A serious drinking problem. He asked me never to tell you about it. He's terribly ashamed, and he's always been afraid that if he kept in touch with you, you'd find out the truth and you wouldn't love him anymore. You see, he wanted you to have wonderful daydreams about him. He wanted you to imagine him as all the things he could never be."

I sat there for a couple of minutes, but I didn't say anything. Finally I went to my room. Mom didn't follow me. I guess she knew I wanted to be alone. I flopped down on my bed and stared at the ceiling. My chest ached so badly it felt as if someone were standing on my heart.

I thought about my father. I was sorry that he had a problem, and I was especially sorry that he was afraid for me to see him the way he really is. He should never have worried that I wouldn't love him if I knew the truth, but I made a secret promise to myself to have only super daydreams about him from now on.

Down deep I guess I had always sort of known that things with my father weren't quite the way I had imagined them. Probably none of the other things were the way I'd imagined them, either. I couldn't believe how gullible I'd been. Just because Melanie was losing weight didn't mean she was anorexic, and how could I ever think that Pink would fool around? He really loves Mom and wants to marry her. I'd always sort of known about my twin, too, but still, I felt a little sad. Now I would never get to meet her or trade places with her or even know her name.

A little while later I looked in my mirror. My twin was there. "Bye," I said, and gave her a little wave. She waved back. I glanced away for a second, and when I looked for her again, she was gone. Only my reflection was looking back at me.

\* \* \*

When the phone rang, I nearly jumped out of my skin. It had to be Randy calling about Taffy Sinclair. I burst out of my room just as Mom picked up the receiver.

"It's for you, Jana. And it's a boy," she said with a big smile.

"Hello?" I said. "Randy?"

"Yeah, it's me. I just got back from Taffy Sinclair's, and she's okay, but, wow, was she mad! She said she had never been so embarrassed and humiliated in her life. She wasn't planning to go back to school again no matter what her parents did to force her. I talked to her, though, and I'm pretty sure she'll be back tomorrow."

I couldn't help feeling relieved. Randy had been a hero just the way I'd known he would be. Then I remembered something.

"But what about the note? Did you ask her about it?"

Randy chuckled. "It has something to do with another soap opera part that she was going to try out for, but she's decided not to. In fact, she's not even going to be on *Interns and Lovers* anymore. She said her parents won't let her because even with Mr. Scott tutoring her, she's getting terrible grades. Her parents said school was more important than being queen of the soaps."

I couldn't help feeling a little smug about that, but at the same time I was feeling guilty again. I knew Randy must be thinking that I was just about the worst person he had ever met.

"And, Jana," he said kind of softly, "I'm sorry I yelled at you. What you did to Taffy was mean, but the more I think about it, the more I really admire you for trying to save her life even though you two aren't friends. Besides, sometimes I can understand why you don't like her. Anyway, I told Taffy what you did. I think that's what changed her mind about going back to school. And one more thing...I was wondering if you'd like to watch me in the football game Saturday afternoon, and then go for pizza with me afterward?"

At first I couldn't believe what he was saying. My heart started pounding like crazy. Randy was finally telling me what he thinks of me. He was saying that he *does* think I'm kind and sensitive and that he's a little bit crazy about me. I remembered what Mom had said about soap operas being intriguing and exciting. Well, this was certainly more intriguing and exciting than any soap opera. I could hardly wait to tell my friends.

"I'd love to go to your game and then out for pizza with you," I said.

After we hung up, I hugged myself. I was so happy I thought I'd die. This was just the beginning for Randy and me. We would be together forever. I closed my eyes. I could see it all.

## ABOUT THE AUTHOR

BETSY HAYNES, the daughter of a former newswoman, began scribbling poetry and short stories as soon as she learned to write. A serious writing career, however, had to wait until after her marriage and the arrival of her two children. But that early practice must have paid off, for within three months Mrs. Haynes had sold her first story. In addition to a number of magazine short stories, and the Taffy Sinclair books Mrs. Haynes is the author of *The Great Mom Swap* and its sequel *The Great Boyfriend Trap*. She lives in Colleyville, Texas, with her children and husband, a businessman who is also an amateur painter and professional cartoonist.

Follow the adventures of Jana and the rest of **THE FABULOUS FIVE** in a new series by Betsy Haynes.

Taffy Sinclair is perfectly gorgeous and totally stuck-up. Ask her rival Jana Morgan or anyone else in the sixth grade of Mark Twain Elementary. Once you meet Taffy, life will **never** be the same.

## Don't Miss Any of the Terrific Taffy Sinclair Titles from Betsy Haynes!

# Skylark is Riding High with Books for Girls Who Love Horses!

# JIM KJELGAARD

In these adventure stories, Jim Kjelgaard shows us the special world of animals, the wilderness, and the bonds between men and dogs. *Irish Red* and *Outlaw Red* are stories about two champion Irish setters. *Snow Dog* shows what happens when a half-wild dog crosses paths with a trapper. The cougar-hunting *Lion Hound* and the greyhound story *Desert Dog* take place in our present-day Southwest. And, *Stormy* is an extraordinary story of a boy and his devoted dog. You'll want to read all these exciting books.

| | |
|---|---|
| ☐ 15578 A NOSE FOR TROUBLE | $2.95 |
| ☐ 15547 HAUNT FOX | $2.75 |
| ☐ 15434 BIG RED | $2.95 |
| ☐ 15546 IRISH RED: SON OF BIG RED | $2.75 |
| ☐ 15427 LION HOUND | $2.95 |
| ☐ 15339 OUTLAW RED | $2.95 |
| ☐ 15560 SNOW DOG | $2.95 |
| ☐ 15468 STORMY | $2.95 |
| ☐ 15466 WILD TREK | $2.95 |

Prices and availability subject to change without notice.

- - - - - - - - - - - - - - - - - - - - - - - - - - - - - -

# Shop at home
# for quality children's books
# *and save money, too.*

Now you can order books for the whole family from Bantam's latest catalog of hundreds of titles including many fine children's books. *And* this special offer gives you an opportunity to purchase a Bantam book for only 50¢. Here's how:

By ordering any five books at the regular price per order, you can also choose any other single book listed (up to a $5.95 value) for just 50¢. Some restrictions do apply, so for further details send for Bantam's catalog of titles today.